Private Research

Also by Sabrina Darby

*The Short and Fascinating Tale of Angelina Whitcombe
On These Silken Sheets*

Private Research

AN EROTIC NOVELLA

SABRINA DARBY

AVON IMPULSE

An Imprint of HarperCollinsPublishers

This is a work of fiction. Names, characters, places, and incidents are products of the author's imagination or are used fictitiously and are not to be construed as real. Any resemblance to actual events, locales, organizations, or persons, living or dead, is entirely coincidental.

Excerpt from *The Governess Club: Claire* copyright © 2013 by Heather Johnson.
Excerpt from *Ashes, Ashes, They All Fall Dead* copyright © 2013 by Lena Diaz.
Excerpt from *The Governess Club: Bonnie* copyright © 2013 by Heather Johnson.

PRIVATE RESEARCH. Copyright © 2013 by Sabrina Darby. All rights reserved under International and Pan-American Copyright Conventions. By payment of the required fees, you have been granted the nonexclusive, nontransferable right to access and read the text of this e-book on screen. No part of this text may be reproduced, transmitted, decompiled, reverse-engineered, or stored in or introduced into any information storage and retrieval system, in any form or by any means, whether electronic or mechanical, now known or hereinafter invented, without the express written permission of HarperCollins e-books.

EPub Edition NOVEMBER 2013 ISBN: 9780062304476
Print Edition ISBN: 9780062304841

10 9 8 7 6 5 4 3 2 1

Acknowledgments

FEW STORIES ARE ever completed without the wonderful input and advice of others. I'd like to thank my editor, Tessa Woodward, and all the people at Avon Impulse who worked on this book. I am indebted to everyone who helped, and in particular to Brenna Aubrey, Amber Anderson, Moriah Jovan, Katharine Ashe, Kate Pearce, Sarah MacLean, Jullie, and, of course, my mother and sister, who are the first readers of nearly everything I write.

Chapter One

IT WAS THE most innocuous of sentences: "A cappuccino, please." Three words, without a verb to ground them, even. Yet, at the sound, my hand stilled midmotion, my own paper coffee cup paused halfway between table and mouth. I looked over to the counter of the cafe. It was midafternoon, quieter than it had been earlier when I'd come in for a quick lunch, and only three people were in line behind the tall, slim-hipped, blond-haired man, whose curve of shoulder and loose-limbed stance struck a chord in me as clearly as his voice.

Of course, it couldn't be. In two years, surely, I would have forgotten the exact tenor of his voice, was confusing some other deep, posh English accent with his. Yet I watched the man, waited for him to turn around, as if there were any significant chance that in a city of 8 million people, I'd run into the one English acquaintance I had. At the National Archives, no less.

At the first glimpse of his profile, I sucked in my breath sharply, nearly dropping my coffee. Then he turned fully, looking around. I watched his gaze pass over me and then snap back in recognition. I was both pleased and terrified. I'd come here to London to put the past behind me, not to face down my demons. I'd been doing rather well these last months, but maybe this was part of some cosmic plan. As my time in England wound down, in order to move forward with my life, I had to come face-to-face with Sebastian Graham again.

"Mina!" He had an impressive way of making his voice heard across the room without shouting, and as he walked toward me, I put my cup down and stood, all too aware that while he looked like a fashionable professional about town, I still looked like a grad student—no makeup, hair pulled back in a ponytail, jeans, sneakers, and a sweater.

"This is a pleasant surprise. Research for your dissertation? Anne Gracechurch, right?"

I nodded, bemused that he remembered a detail from what had surely been a throwaway conversation two years earlier. Of course, I really shouldn't have been. Seb was brilliant, and brilliance wasn't the sort of thing that just faded away.

Neither, apparently, was his ability to make my pulse race a bit faster or to tie up my tongue for a few seconds before I found my stride. He wasn't traditionally handsome, at least not in an American way. Too lean, too angular, hair receding a bit at the temples, and I was fairly certain he was just shy of thirty. But I'd found him attractive from the first moment I'd met him.

I still did.

"That's right. What are you doing here? I mean, at the archives."

"Ah." He shifted and smiled at me, and there was something about that smile that felt wicked and secretive. "A small genealogical project. Mind if I join you?"

I shook my head and sat back down. He pulled out his chair and sat, too, folding his long legs one over the other. Why was that sexy to me?

I focused on his face. He was pale. Much paler than he'd been in New Jersey, like he spent most of his time indoors. Which should have been a turnoff. Yet, despite everything, I sat there imagining him in the kitchen of my apartment in nothing but boxer shorts. Apparently, my memory was as good as his.

And I still remembered the crushing humiliation and disappointment of that last time we'd talked.

"So what have you been up to?" I asked in what I thought was an upbeat tone. Better to take control of this little reunion, keep it to safe topics.

He shrugged. "Work. Quantitative Analysis."

He was downplaying it. Two years ago, far more cockily, he'd shared his future plans to work in finance, to make millions despite the state of the economy, to become one of London's power brokers. (It was why a PhD in mathematics had gone back to school for a one-year Masters in Finance.) But considering how things had been left between us, I didn't feel comfortable teasing him, asking him if he was on track to fulfill his goals of taking over the world, or at least being able to buy it. If the quality of his clothes was any indication, he was. Of course, even back in the States, he'd been well dressed, if more casual.

"And no work today?"

"Saturday," he said simply, and my cheeks grew hot. I'd lost track of time frequently during my research, sometimes startled by a closed business on an unexpected Sunday. "I'm just astounded to see you again," he continued. I didn't miss the way his gaze ran over me, taking everything in. "Two years. Are you still living with Tanya?"

Her name made me wince. In many ways, my old roommate had made my second year of grad school miserable long before Sebastian came into the picture. He didn't know that, but he did know that by saying her name he was hinting at the past.

Did he want to make things even more awkward between us? He had to know it would.

My coffee was done. There was an hour and a half left until the archives closed for the day, and I still had tons to do. Two years ago, I might have been happy to while away the hours discussing everything and anything as I stared into his beautiful pale blue eyes. Now life was different. I was not going to waste away this chance in order to talk for a few more minutes to a guy. Especially this guy.

"No," I said simply, and then slid my laptop from the

table and started to stand. "As fun as catching up is, I have to go back to work."

He stood as well, unfolding himself so effortlessly and elegantly despite being all long limbs. "Listen, I shouldn't have . . ." He stopped talking, and I looked up at him in inquiry. Met his shockingly intense gaze. "Dinner then," he suggested instead of whatever he had been planning to say.

A tremor went through me. Longing. Even desire. He wasn't just some stranger. He was Seb, with whom I'd spent a half dozen or more afternoons talking about all the sorts of things people discuss when they're young, idealistic, and flirting around the attraction they feel. That I had felt.

I could have dinner with an old . . . friend, or I could spend the evening at the inexpensive Indian restaurant around the corner from my cramped, shared flat. They had free wifi and hadn't minded last night when I'd set up shop at one of their back tables as long as I kept ordering appetizers and lassi.

But again, maybe this seemingly chance encounter had happened for a reason and I needed to be a little more open to the vagaries of fate. Maybe it was my opportunity to make some new choices about my life.

"All right," I agreed, embarrassed at the adolescent anticipation fluttering in my belly. "Dinner."

TWENTY MINUTES LATER, ensconced in the private research room with the items I'd requested from the librarian, I stared through the glass wall, barely registering the movement of people—of shapes and colors—across my field of view.

Instead, all I could see was that moment in the middle of a long-ago April, in the kitchen of the grad apartment that I'd shared with Tanya. I was in a tank top and shorts, ready for a late night of studying in bed, or rather, getting ready by preparing a snack of apple slices with almond butter.

"Mina." I could still hear the surprise that had been in Seb's voice when I turned around to find him in my kitchen, in nothing but his blue-and-green-striped boxer shorts. For a moment, I just stared at his chest, at his legs, at a body I had often fantasized about seeing in some distant future. Although, considering the school year was ending in just over a month and he'd be heading back to England, distant could easily have become never.

But there he was in my kitchen, practically naked, with only one possible reason why.

I crumpled a bit inside, disappointed of my vague romantic hopes by his mere presence.

"I didn't know you and Tanya . . ." I trailed off. It was a stupid, revealing thing to say.

We stared at each other silently. He looked almost as shocked as I felt.

"You're taking too long, Seb!" Then Tanya was there, too, totally nude, which wasn't really unusual for her at all. Although I'd only met her in August, by that point in the school year, I'd seen her in all stages of undress. Part of it was her natural nudist tendencies and part was her desire to continually shock me. I was very much looking forward to moving.

His expression had shuttered and he'd turned toward her, reached out an arm, and brought her close. "I didn't realize Mina was your roommate." Which had made it clear to me that, while we'd had some sort of flirtation when we ran into each other on campus or in town, he'd been dating other girls, sleeping with them. I shouldn't have been shocked, but I'd been so innocent back then, so overly romantic.

She looked surprised. "You know each other?" She laughed and looked over at me. "You must spend more time in the library than I would have imagined. Wouldn't think a bookworm like Mina would be so hot, would you?"

I could still remember the heat of my embarrassment, and Tanya doing her usual teasing about my lack of a social life in front of Sebastian. She pulled away from him and came closer to me and to the counter, where she reached up to pull a glass out of the cabinet. Despite myself, I'd stared at her breasts with their pale pink nipples that were practically in my face.

"I've known she's hot for a while." At his words, my gaze snapped back to Sebastian. His familiar face turned foreign. The shared awkwardness was one thing, but with that smirk on his lips, everything had suddenly changed in the room. I felt surrounded, trapped, like the world I knew was spinning out of control. Had he really just said he thought I was hot? Something odd and buoyant simmered in my chest, despite my confusion. "In fact, I was just about to ask if she wanted to join us."

That nascent feeling deflated. I didn't know if he was serious or not. I didn't know which situation would be worse.

The glass Tanya held clattered down on the counter and she spun to face me. I turned from Sebastian's smirk to her vicious expression. I backed up a step before I realized what I was doing.

"Yes . . . join us, Mina," she said in a low, sexy voice. Maybe Sebastian, listening to her, had thought that was what Tanya wanted. But I knew she was taunting me, daring me, that just as she had teased me about being a bookworm, she knew I'd never go in for a threesome. She stepped closer, reached behind me, and stole a slice of my apple before lifting it up toward my lips. "C'mon, take a bite."

I pushed her hand away and slid my plate off the counter, away from her. I forced myself not to run from the room, but as I passed Sebastian, I averted my eyes. I couldn't look at him.

I'd holed up in my room, listening, despite myself, for sounds from Tanya's room, lost in the sinking depression caused by an aborted crush. Maybe half an hour later I heard the front door slam shut, but I didn't know if it was Sebastian alone or both of them. I'd spent the rest of the night trying to understand what had happened, why he'd made that pass. Why he'd done something so crude and so obviously not going to happen. Or maybe he'd thought since I was Tanya's roommate that I'd be up for such a thing.

I'd come up with ways to excuse his behavior, like

perhaps he was fronting for his embarrassment. Furthermore, it wasn't like we'd even been dating, so how could I judge him for sleeping with someone else?

I'd even wondered what would have happened if I'd said yes. I'd wondered that frequently over the following months, and sometimes had wished I had accepted. After all, clearly sex was something he valued more than intellectual discourse. All those conversations we'd had, that slow build of shared intimacy, had been worth nothing.

I didn't know why he'd suggested a threesome, and maybe this night, here in England, was the time to ask, to gain perspective on a moment that had so profoundly impacted my life.

In some irrational way, I'd always seen that night as the beginning of my personal dark ages. Tanya ramped up her evisceration of my life and choices until I was afraid to venture from my room during the few hours I returned to the apartment. I was a coward, she said, even as she followed that up with little details about how Sebastian was in bed. Maybe she was exaggerating for effect, but those details made me flush with embarrassment. With curiosity.

Life had been a spiral down from there to missing the fellowship deadlines necessary to fund my dissertation research and being scolded by my advisor to having to double down with TAing and an outside, part-time job waiting tables to save up enough money to fund myself. Now, here I was in London, determined to prove myself, to complete my research even if I was the only one who cared.

And here *he* was—in a city of millions, in the unlikeliest of places, of course, I'd run into *him*.

I was getting my PhD in English; I knew all about symbolism and foreshadowing. I understood about themes and the way story comes back around. If that night had been the beginning of my dark ages, and this trip to London my chance to come back, then he fit in too. I'd grown so much this last year. I was no longer the naive and romantic student, and Sebastian was a challenge I had to meet.

But in what way? All sorts of wild and ridiculous plans filled my head, but only one seemed to fit the thematic arc of my life.

AT TEN TO five, I retrieved my bag from the locker I'd stashed it in and slid my computer and notebook inside. Despite the mental distraction of seeing Sebastian again, it had been a productive day for research. Although, in some ways, productivity was undefinable. I was like Alice down the rabbit hole, or lost down an infinite number of rabbit holes.

Today, I'd been researching Anne Gracechurch's publisher again and had determined to the best of my knowledge that James Mead, the other author I was researching, seemed to exist only as the author of three books. Although I had diligently pursued the other seventeen James Meads I'd found listed in various registries, I could find no further documentation of his existence .

But as much as people say writing style, syntax, is like

a fingerprint, merely analyzing the text of a Mead work and a Gracechurch work side by side, or fed through a computer program (as I had), wouldn't be enough for my dissertation. Not in the cutthroat world of academics. Not if I wanted a tenure-track position in the future, or at least the option to pursue one. For that, I needed proof. I needed at least one more link other than the fact that they had shared a publisher a good portion of writers at the time had also used.

Since arriving in London four months earlier, I'd filled in the gaps of Anne's genealogy, charted the connections she'd had with anyone during her lifetime, contacted or attempted to contact everyone on my list. I'd determined the locations of her known correspondence and visited archives across the country, poring over old documents. It was painstaking work and easy to get lost in the depths of it. Research in the day, take copies home and research in the evening.

Solitary work, other than the conversations with archivists, librarians, and researchers, or with clerks at grocery stores and baristas at coffee shops, where I ordered the cheapest drink just to use the wifi. It was as if I'd drained myself socially, exorcised the overly extroverted poltergeist who had taken over my body for a while.

And I was having dinner with Sebastian Graham. Wasting an evening better spent organizing my notes and thoughts so that I could focus the next day's research.

But I was torn between the urge to run far away from him and everything I'd rejected the day I boarded the plane for England, and the desire to use this encounter as another line drawn in the sand. Satisfy that long-held curiosity and desire. Sleep with him even. Hair of the dog, in a way.

I met him outside the front doors of the archives. He was standing there, legs slightly parted, staring out into the distance, one hand in his pocket and the other holding a folded stack of papers, the results of whatever genealogical research he had done in the afternoon. His stance was so American, but maybe that was the eleven years he had spent in the States.

He looked as good in his jacket and slacks from the back as he had from the front. Only, from this vantage point I could admire his slim-hipped elegance, the tension of his body hinting at strength. Six-foot-one, if I recalled correctly. Not so tall, really, but he gave the impression of being taller than he was.

"So . . ." I said when I stood beside him, interrupting whatever thoughts had consumed him. He looked down at me and I was lost for a moment in pale blue eyes that made him so real and so known to me. Despite two years. Despite the past. Or maybe because of the past.

A pleasurable shiver rushed through my body, settled hot and full between my legs, and I shifted where I stood.

"Early for food," he said. "A drink?"

A drink was exactly what I needed.

I nodded and followed him to his car. It was a pleasure to be able to stash my bag in the trunk, or rather the *boot* as he called it and relax into a relatively comfortable seat. As convenient as the underground system was, I'd grown up with wide, open spaces and had an instinctive aversion to small, crowded ones.

We didn't drive very far, and in those few minutes there was only idle chitchat: Sebastian asking when I'd arrived and if I'd just been working since, me answering and staring out the window at the landscape, taking in the view I'd missed on the way out to Kew. Then we fell into silence.

The plan that I had formulated at the archives ricocheted in my head. I'd decided that, since he was the one who had prompted my ill-advised phase of sleeping around and clearly it was fate that had thrown us together once again, I should have sex with him. English major that I had been, I still saw the world in terms of themes and circles, subplots and motifs. Yet, I hardly knew him and had absolutely nothing to say to him. But if there was anything I'd learned in the past two years, it was that casual sex didn't need a mental connection.

What it needed was lubrication of the alcoholic kind.

We ended up at a pub maybe ten minutes from the archives. Sebastian said it was fairly traditional, and at just after five, it was still quiet.

We sat inside at a corner table. Ordered our drinks.

"It's hard to believe . . . two years," he started, and it was, almost exactly. The last time I'd seen him had been at the very end of the semester, out on the bright green lawn. We hadn't talked. When he'd seemed like he was going to approach me, I'd averted my eyes and headed off in the other direction. Maybe if I'd known he was leaving only a few days later, I would have waited, braved the awkward conversation.

"Longer than we even knew each other," I added with a laugh. Diminishing those conversations and the four months of growing friendship.

"And here we are now."

As far as conversations went, it was hardly scintillating. Instead, it was awkward talking around the subject. I was on edge, wanting to say something, thinking it better that I didn't. Or thinking that maybe this conversation would be easier after we'd had that drink.

Did I really want to talk about it?

Not really. What I wanted to do was breach this strange wall between us, take things physical even though it was still light outside, still afternoon more than evening.

The waitress brought us our drinks and I reached for mine gratefully. Sebastian ordered another round for us both.

"So tell me about your research," he said suddenly, as if we hadn't been on the edge of a different conversation.

It wasn't easy switching tracks that fast, but I had my spiel ready, the same speech I'd given to my advisor last year. "I'm not certain what I've already told you about Anne Gracechurch."

"She wrote around the same time as the Brontës, was popular but drifted into obscurity? I think you said she wrote seventeen novels. Whatever would be pulp fiction for the time."

Again, I was startled by how much he remembered.

"Twenty," I corrected. "Or rather, I *believe* she wrote twenty. And my goal is to prove it."

He took another gulp of his ale like it was water. It was nearly all gone while half my vodka martini was still there. I sipped at it again. When the waiter brought our next set of drinks, I swallowed down the one in my hand.

"So, you found some mention of three other books. Is that enough for a dissertation?"

"If everyone thinks those three books written by a man?"

He nodded in appreciation. I could see the light of intellectual interest in his eyes. "How do you intend to prove it?"

"One aspect is the syntax, the style. A line-by-line comparison shows a tremendous similarity. This past fall, I did an in-depth study of the text of both authors, and I talked to forensic linguists who concur. But that isn't enough. I need to show a physical link between them. A letter to the printer or some reference somewhere. Proof that James Mead absolutely didn't exist other than on the frontispiece of those three books. Which is what I've been doing since January. Or trying to do."

"January," he repeated.

"Yeah. I leave in two weeks."

He looked as if he was going to say something else about it, but with one vodka martini under my figurative belt and another dangerously close to sloshing over the rim in my unsteady grip, I didn't want to talk about the research anymore. As usually happened when the alcohol took hold, I had a decidedly oral fixation. And I was studying Sebastian with a new appreciation for his features, the slight shadow under his cheekbones, the generous length of his thin lips. It would take me days to fully explore his body with my mouth, with my tongue. Kissing him would be—

"Not very much time at all." I met his eyes, startled that he'd read my thoughts. "Did you find your link?" I inched closer to him. His eyes narrowed in something that maybe was confusion. Which made me stop. Rethink.

Then I laughed, at myself, at the conversation, at how close I'd come to jumping the gun on this.

He raised an eyebrow, and I put my drink down. Searched for an excuse.

"Maybe we'd better order some food," I said with an apologetic shrug.

"Americans don't know how to drink," he said, shaking his head.

"Or maybe we do." I stared into my glass, finger running along the rim. "In any event, I haven't found it yet. The link. Proof."

At Sebastian's beckoning gesture, the waitress came by and we ordered.

"And what if you don't find it?"

I looked back up at him again. Found him watching me attentively.

"Then I adjust, adapt. Simply because I want something to be one way doesn't mean it is." Only, I wasn't talking about the work. I was talking about Sebastian and the way I'd felt about him. About my romantic ideals, my dreams of love and even an ephemeral thought of white dresses and babies, which had been shattered so easily, first casually by him and then ruthlessly by me.

Was my plan for the evening another ruthless attack on myself, or was it really the right thing to do? Healing in a twisted way?

"That's an excellent perspective to have," he said, clearly missing the subtext. "Adaptability is the key to success."

I laughed. "I'd bet you haven't had to adapt to failure ever."

"Ah, but I have."

"Sebastian Graham, you seem like the type to have what you want fall into your lap." Even as I spoke, I knew it was the alcohol that made me so forward, so flirtatious. The alcohol and the fact that I had liked him once upon a time.

"*You* didn't."

I froze for a moment, and then smiled, reaching for my drink. I held it up as if I were about to make a toast.

"We could remedy that."

His eyes widened slightly before narrowing, and a small line creased his forehead.

I'd shocked him. Good. Because he'd shocked me, too, by admitting he'd wanted me. Or maybe he'd wanted a threesome.

"Mina." All humor fled his voice and in the face of that seriousness, I downed the rest of my drink fast, even though I knew I should stop. If the food didn't come soon, I'd be a mess. "I know I didn't handle things well that night.

"I suppose I thought after seeing me with Tanya . . . I was trying to . . ."

"You don't have to explain," I interrupted. Thankfully, the waitress seemed to realize a diversion was necessary for my sanity. She slid our plates in front of us before disappearing again.

"But I do," he insisted. "It was an awkward situation, and I figured I'd lost any chance with you anyway—"

"Sebastian, your point is made," I said quickly, cutting him off again. I no longer wanted to hear his explanation, to have to think about what it meant for my life, for the choices I'd made. I was so tired of analyzing everything. He had insisted on dinner, and therefore, tonight, he was simply a means to an end. "You have had to struggle against adversity in your life."

He laughed, and I laughed, too, before pointing to the television screen hanging from the ceiling and asking about the soccer game that was playing. He paused for the briefest moment before answering my question, and I hoped he wouldn't press the issue. He didn't. Instead, I listened to his patter, relieved that he seemed willing to follow my lead.

My lead. This time I was in charge. I wasn't the same girl who'd run from the kitchen in embarrassment, and I'd meant what I'd said so carelessly a few minutes earlier. There was one way to make this chance encounter meaningful. One way to close the circle.

As we ate our food, talked about sports and team rivalries, my focus was on the very near future. On getting Sebastian Graham into bed.

Chapter Two

WE LEFT SHORTLY after finishing our meals. The night was chilly, a mist in the air, despite it being spring.

"Where are you staying?" he asked as we walked toward his car. He played with his keys in his hand and the sound of their jangling was loud in the relatively quiet neighborhood.

"So that's it?" I asked. "Just dinner? Old school chums catching up? As if we both aren't curious what it would have been like between us?"

"I didn't think . . ." I'd caught him by surprise. Sebastian stood on the sidewalk, keys dangling from his finger. He watched me carefully, assessing, maybe realizing that I'd meant what I said earlier in the pub, that this night could go differently than he'd imagined.

"Then don't think," I interrupted, moving closer. I'd learned a lot about seduction in the last two years. I'd learned that conversation was like music, physical space a medium to play with. As I stepped close, merely a centimeter between us, his breath caught. I lifted up on my toes and closed that infinitesimal space with the press of my body against his, enjoying the delicious electricity of first contact as I looked up into his face and willed him to kiss me.

He answered, and I knew his heat an instant before the touch of his lips, the wrap of his arms around me, the sensation of being completely taken over by a man who understood exactly what he was doing. I was held up by his arms and lost in the pleasure that unfurled down my body in increasingly potent tendrils.

I pressed closer to him, feeling the strength of his body beneath his suit, the heat of his growing erection against my hip. Simply the knowledge of that hardness made me shiver with longing, made me feel empty and desirous between my legs.

"Your place," I murmured, breaking away just enough to enunciate the words.

He lifted his hands to my face and stared down at me, his gaze intense. Then he nodded and let me go.

I was giddy inside as he opened the car door, watched me slide in and then shut the door behind me. In the silent emptiness of the car as I waited for him to round it and join me, I envisioned his naked form with nearly breathless anticipation.

Then he was with me again, his gaze hot with erotic promise, and I shifted in the seat, damp and needy.

The fifteen-minute drive across the city was a tense, silent blur. Light washed over us—blue, red, green, and white. The reflection of cars and streetlights shone off surfaces, off the watch on Sebastian's wrist, which I hadn't noticed earlier but did during my desirous study of his hands.

"Are you sure?" he asked at one point. In answer, I placed my own hand on his thigh, stroking teasingly across the lightweight wool blend, my touch firm enough to feel the muscle beneath. He glanced at me out of the corner of his eye, the end of his lips quirked up slightly. I kept my hand there, stroking, inching ever so slightly higher. Knowing that I affected him, that I could make him do what I wanted, aroused me even more.

He lived in a modern building that had sprouted up during the renovation of the King's Cross area, the garage and convenience of the underground within a few blocks being the deciding factors.

His one-bedroom flat wasn't drastically different from anything I'd seen in America and had all the modern conveniences I'd been told not to expect in England, like air-conditioning, a decent-sized refrigerator, and cabinets in the bathroom. Certainly, they weren't present in my flat.

"Would you like a drink?" he asked, as he shrugged out of his coat and hung it over a chair at the dining table. This was that moment of starting over again, getting back into the mood after an extended, enforced break.

"Yes," I agreed, following him closely, so that when he turned around in the small kitchen, he turned into my arms. He had a sexy, somewhat cocky smile, and I lifted up on my toes to meet it with my lips. Contact. Stunning and drugging. His mouth became my world and I wrapped my arms around his neck to get closer. His hands grasped my hips, lifted me against him. I was only half-aware that he was moving me until I was perched on the counter, legs wrapped around him, head against the cupboard.

I drank him in, the taste of his skin, the feel of his lips, his tongue. And between my legs, through the layers of cloth—my jeans and his trousers—he was hard and pressing against me.

One hand threaded through the hair at the back of his head and with the other I touched his skin, my thumb exploring the texture of his jaw, his cheek, the slight roughness of the skin at the end of the day. The pads of my fingers tingled with sensation.

He was my drink. His touch and his scent made me dizzy, intoxicated.

"Too many clothes," he muttered. And I had to agree. He pulled at my sweater, lifting it up, and I raised my arms to help him. I reached for the buttons on his shirt, but he stopped me, his warm hands on the bare skin of my arms, and me still, his eyes running over me. I loved that expression on his face, so intense and filled with desire.

He reached for my tank top, slid it up over my body, peeling my clothes like I was a Christmas gift.

I was suddenly aware of my plain grey cotton underwire bra. When I'd put it on that morning, I hadn't imagined anyone other than me seeing it. He ran his thumbs over the curves of my breasts above the cups of the bra.

Then the bra itself didn't matter anymore. What mattered was the way he was pulling the cloth down, exposing me fully to his view. I shivered as cooler air hit my nipples, and his thumb circled where the flesh stood stiff.

He leaned forward again, arms circling me to unhook my bra. He slipped it off me and threw it . . . somewhere. His hands were back, this time cradling my head just before his lips found mine again. My naked breasts pressed hard against his chest. The smooth fabric of his shirt teased me, made my skin tingle. But I wanted more. I reached between us and started unbuttoning his shirt. This time, he didn't stop me. I yanked the cloth free of his pants and delved underneath, feeling with my hands what I wanted to see later with my eyes. I wrapped my arms around him, caressing his back, naked skin to naked skin, and felt the briefest moment of peace before the sharpness of desire took over again.

He broke the kiss. "Let's move into the bedroom." He didn't wait for me to respond, just lifted me off the counter, and I slid down his body slowly, looking up at him in that semistupor of unfulfilled desire.

I followed him across the apartment. His bedroom was big, by London standards. He had what looked like a queen-size bed, but all I knew was that it was far bigger than my single back at the flat.

But there would be time for looking at furniture and decorations later. What I wanted was the half-dressed male body standing in front of me. I reached for his belt buckle, slid the leather tongue out, and then focused on the fastening of his pants. Maybe I was too slow, fumbling too much, because he took over. I moved on to my own jeans, unbuttoning, unzipping, and then pushing them down my legs and off.

We stood there, me in my panties, he in his boxer shorts, staring at each other.

For a moment I was transported back to the kitchen of my old grad apartment. Only, this time, there was no Tanya. This time, I was saying yes.

Except...

"Seb, we should talk."

He took a deep breath. "Okay. I agree."

It was all too clear he thought I wanted to discuss the past when that was the last thing I wanted to talk about.

"No," I corrected with a small laugh. "About safe sex . . ." The words sounded so formal, but I'd had this conversation dozens of times over the last two years. Not that the conversation alone meant anything but... it was more than nothing.

"Right." He laughed too, as if he were nervous, and shook his head. Then he spoke briskly. "I've been tested fairly recently. It's been months since I've been with anyone. I can't be 100 percent sure, but I'm negative for everything."

Relief swept through me, except...

"Me, too, but I can't say for sure either."

His eyebrow rose, and I stared straight back at him, challenging that doubtful expression with my own amused little smile. He only knew the old Mina, the shocked little innocent. I liked that this time he was the one who was surprised.

Finally, his lips curved up.

"It sounds like we've minimized risk, and condoms should minimize it more."

Minimized risk. Risk management was part of his job after all. Yet, even if he was right, it sounded so odd. But . . . I didn't want to think about that anymore. I wanted *him*.

I stepped forward and rose onto my toes to reach his face, wrapping one hand behind his head to bring him down the few inches I needed. Any momentum we might have lost during the brief conversation was recovered in an instant. He was hard against me everywhere, especially *there*, where fabric kept us from moving too fast.

"Mina, fuck," he whispered against my lips, and then lifted me up and turned us around. The room spun until I was flat on my back on the bed and he was climbing on top of me, pressing himself against me, the rigid length of him rubbing back and forth between my legs even as his mouth opened hot and electrifying on my neck. I gasped as he devoured me, his lips and tongue moving across my skin like wicked things, leaving a burning trail of wet fire.

My arms flopped to my sides under the sensual onslaught and I simply *felt*.

But when his lips closed over one of my nipples, I gasped again and reached for him, to feel his skin under my hands, to say something about how right it was when, with my own mouth, it was all I could do to breathe.

And his hands . . . they were moving everywhere his mouth was not, down my waist, to my hips, tugging on my underwear, until he finally moved away for the briefest moment to pull them off completely.

Then his body was back between my legs, his mouth on the planes of my abdomen, and anticipation for the inevitable goal of his methodical progress down my body had me oversensitized and trembling at every touch.

I wanted his mouth on me, and suddenly it was there, at the center of sensation, gentle and exploring. I heard myself moaning unconsciously, as if it weren't me. He found the right rhythm, the right everything.

"Yes. There," I said on a breath, as the swirl of sensation started rising on the path that was so familiar yet, at the same time, always new.

I was close, so close, and my whole body tensed. I fell over the peak, opening up, my hips moving, as I cried out, reaching for him.

But he made his way back up my body slowly, and every place his mouth touched made me shudder again. Too much, but not enough. I wanted him inside me. I reached for him and found he'd shed the barrier of his boxer shorts. I sighed as my hand closed around the hard length of him, learning for the first time his shape and texture.

When his lips reached my neck, he leaned over to his left, to the side table, and slid open a drawer. Then he was back, tearing the condom wrapper. He paused as I stroked him, eyes closing.

I watched his face, trying to learn what he liked best. Clearly, he enjoyed what I was doing, but he opened his eyes and moved away from me. I looked on hungrily as he rolled the condom down his penis, which was thick and straight and ridiculously gorgeous.

He leaned over me again, mouth against my ear. I parted my legs farther, urging him inward. When his hips pressed forward, I held my breath at the first touch of him against me. He slid forward easily, deliciously, stretching me, and I wrapped my legs around his hips, bringing him deeper.

He pulled out slowly, and then, just as slowly, thrust back in, and then again. And again. Each stroke teased my sensitive flesh and brought me higher and higher in that spiraling up of sensation. We both grew more desperate—hands and mouths sliding down skin, massaging, pulling, faster and faster until he wasn't slow and gentle anymore. Until I climaxed in a rush of movement, gasping, "Oh my God."

My body floated around his as he moved faster, seeking his pleasure. He stiffened over me, his lips drawn back, neck arched, and he cried out, too, his cry deeper, more guttural, like it had been drawn out from the deepest part of his body. He fell forward. With him heavy on my body, his lips open against my neck, I clung to him still, my legs tight, my hands stroking down the now-relaxed muscles of his back.

"I FIGURED YOU'D be good in bed, experienced," I said, after he'd rolled to the side and my mind had gathered any sense of clarity. Either he was simply skilled at sex, or the attraction between us was like nothing I'd ever felt with anyone else. Maybe both.

"I'll take good. As for the rest . . ." He laughed. "I suppose you'd think that, considering, but really, I haven't had time to do much of anything the last two years, including date. I work for an American firm, which means longer American hours, but it's higher pay and a position closer to the action."

I didn't understand the specifics of that.

"To the money," he clarified. "In this field, if you're ambitious, if you can take the stress, you want to be as close to the money as possible."

I could have asked him to explain, and once I would have, would have wanted to understand every minute detail of the work Sebastian did. I probably would have gone home and searched "quantitative analysis" just so I could understand the jargon, could have educated conversations with him about something that so obviously was of interest. In fact, I'd done a bit of that when we'd first met, which was the only reason I had any idea what investment banks and hedge funds did, what quantitative analysis entailed.

But no more. In another few minutes, I'd slink out of this bed and back into my clothes. As much as I'd enjoyed these last hours, I'd leave this night and Sebastian behind. I had no need to fill my brain with details that didn't matter.

What did matter? I reached out and rested a fingertip on his hip, stroked the hollow there, and then down, skimming the muscle, deliberating if I wanted another round. Good-bye sex.

"You have time for the gym," I teased, pointing out his lean physique.

"There's a twenty-four-hour room in the building," he said with a slight laugh.

It wasn't much of a deliberation. Of course, I wanted sex again. My body now knew what it was like to have his inside it, to be stretched and fitted to him, to wrap legs around hips. I wanted more. I'd accepted this one night with him as a fitting punctuation mark, a comma between my old life and my new, and I had no doubt I should make the most of it.

I closed my hand over the awakening length of his penis. I yearned to know the feel of him in my mouth, but not when he likely still tasted of sex and latex. He hardened under the movements of my hand and then shifted over me, parting my legs with his knees. His fingers eased open my flesh, searching for a readiness that was there. He paused for a new condom and then, no foreplay, no lingering touches, simply Sebastian inside me, moving, and me reveling in it.

We didn't talk or make a sound other than the heaviness of our breaths. I arched against him, searching for the friction that I craved. He stopped, pulled out, and rolled onto his back, bringing me with him.

We still didn't speak as I lowered myself on him, enjoying that sharp sensation anew from this different angle, and then his fingers were on me, touching me as we moved, manipulating me perfectly.

I would never have imagined I'd be here, Sebastian inside me, after everything that had happened. I'd told myself I was done with sleeping around and trying to prove to myself that I was worldly and unafraid. But apparently this, this finale, was what I needed to set my life back on track. Except there would be no *finale* if I kept thinking.

I focused on Sebastian instead, on the texture of his skin under my fingertips, on the smooth thrusting, the sounds of growing pleasure, the echo of that inside my body. He leaned up, mouth closing over one of my nipples, and I gasped. Electric. Sharp.

Chapter Three

DARKNESS. WARMTH OF covers and lingering dreams that I didn't want to leave. But something niggled at me, a sense that I had to be awake, that I had things to do. I stretched my body in luxurious denial. And hit a leg. A warm, hairy...

Sebastian.

The previous night came back to me in a rush. I was wide-awake with no idea what time it was. With the window shades tightly drawn, I could only tell that there was a hint of light beyond, filtering through. Had I slept away one of my few precious days here in England? Disgust prompted me out of the bed despite the niggling desire to see if what had been so amazing at night, after several drinks, was equally powerful in the sober day.

I searched in the dim light for my clothes. Found my jeans. I was fairly certain my sweater, tank, and bra would be in the living room. What I couldn't find was my underwear. I needed more light. Instead, I stole from the room and went to the bathroom to put myself in some semblance of order.

In the bright light of the bathroom, I stared at myself in the mirror. I looked . . . not just bed rumpled from the night, brown hair hopelessly tangled, but fucked. No, not just fucked . . . since I'd had more than my fair share of sexual encounters over the last two years, but satisfied, my nude body a bit lusher than the day before.

Yeah. Sebastian Graham rocked in bed. Moist heat gathered between my legs at the mere thought.

Twelve days, I reminded myself. I could fantasize about the sex tonight in my own bed. Not that the thin walls of the flat were conducive to masturbation (I could always hear my flatmates when they had girls over). But I didn't need to waste time.

I also didn't need to pass up the chance to shower in an immaculate and spacious bathroom. He had a stack of what I assumed were clean towels inside a cabinet in the corner, so I pulled one out. I wasn't the sort to root around in a guy's home in order to know more about him—I completely believe in privacy—but co-opting items to clean up the morning after? Totally fair game.

I helped myself to his toiletries: shampoo, conditioner, a rather nice facial cleaner, some toothpaste on my finger. My hair creamy with conditioner, I stood in the bathtub and let the hot water flow over my body. It felt so good.

Normally, the morning after a one-night stand—and by then, I'd had my fair share—I would have run away as fast as possible, and not because of the guilt over wasting my precious work time. No, what had made me flee was having to look at myself, was knowing that I was deliberately making myself into Sebastian and Tanya, people for whom casual sex was preferred over any sort of real relationship. Not that I'd realized it on those mornings with any conscious thought. Rather, it had been months later, when I'd struggled to put my life back on track, that I'd psychoanalyzed myself, realized I'd been reshaping myself in the image of someone who had hurt me, as if that could protect me against further hurt.

But today I didn't feel guilty about the sex. Which unsettled me even more.

Through the glass shower doors, I saw him watching me. He was naked and completely, unmistakably turned on. He offered me a crooked little smile and reached for the handle of the door.

"I thought for a moment you'd left. Then I found your underwear by the bed and heard the shower," he said. "Mind if I join you?" He actually waited for an answer, letting the cooler air from outside the shower breeze in.

"It's getting late, isn't it?"

"Just after eight." Not nearly as late as I'd feared. "Late for a workday, but it's Sunday."

Still a workday for me, but maybe I could spare fifteen extra minutes. Especially as the archives weren't open today. Or tomorrow.

I lifted my chin in invitation. An instant later, the shower wasn't nearly as spacious as it had felt. He reached for me, pulled me wet and soapy against his body. His erection was hot and firm against my stomach.

"Turn around," he suggested. I turned obediently, as if the only thing that mattered was this moment here with him in the shower, two naked beings fairly buzzing with attraction. I closed my eyes against the spray of the shower as his hands spread through my still-conditioner-lathered hair. His expertise appeared to extend to scalp massages as well.

We washed each other's bodies slowly, lingeringly. Then he bent his head, his lips opening mine with his own in a melting kiss. Water dripped from his hair onto my forehead as the showerhead sprayed against my backside. I leaned into him, hungry for his taste. While his hand played between my legs, his fingers sliding shallowly across the groove of my sex, I grasped him in my hand, studying the thickness, the length, the shape under my palm.

I slid down his body until I was on my knees in the tub in front of him, until his erect penis was perfectly in line with my lips. I took him again in my hand and pressed my lips softly to his skin. He sucked in a breath. The sound empowered me.

I licked the head greedily, loving the soft, velvety feel of him under my tongue, the ridge where the head of his cock met the shaft. I sucked him into my mouth, tongue swirling, enjoying the salty taste of his precum and the fullness of him inside my mouth, which sent a fresh surge of heat through my body. Sensation gathered in my nipples, between my legs.

My lips were on sensory overload, everything centered there. I relaxed my mouth a bit to slide over him, take him deeper, start the slow, regular rhythm that echoed sex. I clutched his buttocks in my hands and savored his groan as I took him in completely for just a moment before retreat. He had a beautiful, delicious cock.

I picked up my pace. I was past my own desire. All I wanted was to give him pleasure, to bring him to orgasm inside my mouth, to feel the triumph of taking him in that way, of swallowing a part of him. His hands threaded through my hair, clutching at my scalp, and I reveled in the feel of his restrained strength. Some wild part of me wanted him to take over, hold me tight and use me, but his firm touch was gentle, letting me have control.

I lost any sense of time in the motion, in the focus on tensing my lips just the right amount around him, on doing everything I could to please him. I slid one hand between his legs and stroked the warm sacs there, finding the places that seemed most sensitive.

He jerked against me, his grip tightening as he clutched me to him, emptying himself in my mouth, down my throat. I savored his strength, savored that moment of feeling powerless against his pleasure.

I slid back slightly, swallowing, before moving forward again and sucking his now-softer length inside. I licked him slowly, loving the tremors of his body, until he pulled me up.

He kissed me hot and openmouthed, and my lips were slack against his but ready for the onslaught. As he ravished my mouth, his hands roamed down over my body, lifting my breasts, then one hand lower, fingers thrusting almost roughly into me. I gasped, spreading my legs wider.

"That's it," he urged softly against my mouth. "Open up for me."

Open for him. I'd take all of him, everything he had. I wanted him to fuck me and fill me up, but there was no way he'd be ready for that again so soon.

I barely registered the squeak of the plumbing as he turned off the shower, but I did feel the sudden breeze of air breaking through the steam. Then his hot mouth moving down my body, to my neck, my clavicle, my breasts. As he came lower, the thrusts of his fingers grew shallower, teasing me, until he was kneeling in front of me, thumbs spreading me open before him, stroking.

I was shivering uncontrollably, from his touch, from the chill, from the anticipation of knowing in just a moment more—

His mouth closed on me, hot and perfect. I could have died then and there from the exquisite pleasure of that touch. He knew how to use his lips and his tongue. He knew what to do to me. Then his fingers were back, three of them filling me where I was wet and hungry. I clutched at his shoulders, my knees weak.

I looked down at him, at his head buried in the junction of my legs, mouth on my sex. *Sebastian.*

The sensation kept rising, rising, until I bucked against him, waves overtaking me. I shook in his arms as explosions rocked through my body, and inside I pulsed around his fingers. Still, he sucked on me, his tongue lapping at my inner folds, lingeringly, soothingly.

Finally, he lifted his head away, and I slid down. He pulled me to him, until we were both lying in the tub, side by side, legs entangled.

I shuddered again with a final release and was still, head against his chest.

"I need to work," I said after a long silence, although my body felt boneless and I didn't want to move. But it was important to get going. I'd indulged a little bit more, but this was, for all intents and purposes, a one-night stand. Lingering had no purpose.

"Mmm." He lifted his hand to my breast and ran a finger around the nipple. Even sated as I was, I wanted more of that touch. "Can you work from here?" he asked, as if there were no question that his plan, so boldly stated, would be undertaken. "There's a great cafe down the street for breakfast, then maybe,"—he pulled on my nipple gently—"I can convince you to take a midafternoon break."

Inwardly, I froze. Was he expecting that this would go on? That I'd spend more precious minutes of my research trip having sex with him? Having dinners and breakfasts and . . .

That might have sounded good to me in the past, but now I was far more realistic. I understood what this was between us and I knew my priorities.

"Listen, Seb," I said, closing my legs finally and sitting up. "This was fun, but I don't really have time for a repeat performance."

He closed his eyes. I wondered for a moment at the thoughts hidden behind his still features. Then those pale blue eyes focused on me, and he smirked. "Yes, it was fun, and as much as I *would* love a repeat, and very much regret that we didn't run into each other a few months ago, I have something else I want to talk about."

I was curious what he wanted to discuss if not sex. After all, pretty much the entirety of our relationship, at least the part that had any lasting relevance, revolved around sex in some way. Him propositioning me or me propositioning him.

"I was wondering, actually, if you'd be willing to help me with some of my research. I've never undertaken anything of the like, and I rather suspect you'd have a bit more success than I. I've come up against some dead ends."

"Your genealogy research?" I prodded, looking at him skeptically. Not that I was actually considering it. With less than two weeks left to conduct my own research, I could hardly take on another project. Especially a project that would require me to be in continual contact with Sebastian. All I'd ever think about would be sex, which was already at the forefront of my mind, lying here naked, wanting him again.

He reached out and stroked the hair between my legs with the back of his hand, as if it were natural that he would touch me so familiarly, in the middle of a conversation that was supposedly not about sex. He tugged lightly on the hair, and I had to force myself not to close my eyes and give in.

I didn't make him move his hand.

"It involves genealogy," he amended. "It's a bit more

complicated than that. I'm trying to hunt down the history of a private club to which my grandfather belonged."

Brooks's, White's, Boodle's—names of old, established gentleman's clubs instantly filled my mind. But the history of most of those was well documented, so that was unlikely. Maybe it was something closer to the Lunar Society, the group of late-eighteenth-century intellectuals who had met on the full moon of every month to exchange information about their research. Something casual, only mentioned in letters and journal entries.

His thumb found my clit, which was still sensitive from the attention of his mouth. I shuddered and shifted away from the almost painful sensation. There, languor gone. I twisted onto my side, disentangling from him, and pulled the towel down from the shower rod.

"I'm sure it's a fascinating story, Seb," I said, getting to my feet, "but I doubt I'll have time to take on more work. I only have these next twelve days to do my own research. If you need help, why don't you hire a researcher?"

Towel wrapped around me, I stepped out of the shower. Then I picked up the pile of my clothing.

He was standing outside now, too, naked still, and so comfortable in his nakedness despite the water dripping down his skin. I could stare at him all day, explore his body, run my tongue down his stomach, his legs, down every indent of muscle. I thrust one of the extra towels at him.

"I thought about it," he admitted as he followed me into his bedroom. "But some of my family history is . . . sensitive. I'd rather not entrust it to a stranger."

He'd opened the window shades and, in the much brighter light of day, I could see my errant underwear on the floor at the foot of the bed.

He didn't consider me to be a stranger.

Once, I wouldn't have considered him one either. But that night had made me rethink everything I thought I knew. Made me realize I was crushing on a figment of my own imagination.

I dropped my clothes and the towel on the bed and reached for my underwear. I supposed that after the night we had, we at least knew each other's bodies better.

He put clothes on as well, but these, a button-down shirt and jeans, were much more casual than those of the day before, more the way he would have dressed back at school.

"Maybe I can give you a few pointers," I found myself saying, despite everything, despite how bad an idea it was to do anything but leave. After all, to help, I'd need to know more about the club, about what he knew so far and what steps he'd taken. I could envision a half-hour conversation devolving into a several-hour one, the same way my quick shower had resulted in oral sex before breakfast.

"No need." He brushed it off with a devastating smile. "I'll muddle through. Come, I'll drive you back to your flat."

Chapter Four

WE ENDED UP grabbing surprisingly good coffees downstairs at the coffee shop on the corner for the drive across town. It should have been awkward—we'd had a one-night stand, and I'd rejected his request for help—but it wasn't. Instead, we talked about the city. He acted like the consummate tour guide, telling me about the streets we passed and the neighborhoods. Pointing out any historical sites. Which was nice because I hadn't spent much time sightseeing, though I had promised myself a few days of fun activities at the end of the trip if I met my goals.

It was almost as if that night in New Jersey had never happened. Like we were simply two people who had gravitated toward each other in the hallways, sat together on benches. And I wanted him again. Wanted to go back to his apartment and stay there indefinitely, as if the rest of the world and time didn't exist. Except,

I wasn't that same overly romantic Anglophile, swept away by an appealing accent, a charming smile, and a few common interests.

So instead, in the narrow private room that I'd rented in a three-bedroom flat of graduate students and postdocs, I placed my backpack on the floor and lay down on the bed, unzipped my jeans, and slid my hand down. After the previous night I should have been satisfied, but it was like I'd reawakened my appetite for sex. I knew I had work to do, but I wouldn't be able to concentrate unless I burned off this extra tension. I ran my other hand over my body, then pushed up my shirt and moved my bra aside so that I could cup my bare breast the way he had. As my fingers stroked fast, in a rhythm I knew well, I thought of him filling my mouth, filling me, almost as if he could do both at once.

I came fast and hard, bucking against the bed and moaning out loud, every bit of my body down to my toes tingling with the force of the orgasm. I pulled my hand from my crotch, yanked my shirt down, and flipped onto my side, staring at the wall.

All right, then. Itch satisfied. Work time.

AFTER CHANGING INTO fresh, comfortable clothing, opening my computer and the document copies I'd gathered the previous day and spreading everything out on the bed, I reached for my cell phone instead. I'd used it sparingly over the last four months as, even with an international plan and a local sim card, I couldn't afford the pay-by-the-minute rates. Instead, my interactions with family and friends were primarily via e-mail, Internet calls, and IMs.

But I needed to talk to someone.

I dialed Sophie's number, only realizing when she answered with a sleep-roughened voice, that I'd called her at 5 A.M. on Sunday morning, New York time.

"Oh God. I'm sorry, Sophie. I'll call back later."

"Mina? Is that you? What's wrong?"

"Nothing. I just forgot about the time difference for a moment. I'll call back later." I hung up and tossed the phone on the bed. Wiped the back of my hand across my eyes.

All right, time to focus.

Someone knocked on my door. Taking a deep breath, I stood up, turned the lock, and opened it.

Jens, the chemistry postdoc from Germany, stood out there, grinning at me. He was a nice enough guy who often invited me out drinking with his friends.

"Out all night?"

"Bumped into an old friend," I said tightly, knowing I had to say something if I didn't want to deal with winks and teasing. Especially considering Jens had hit on me several times already. Even though he was attractive and funny and I likely would have slept with him last year, I'd been determined to focus on my research.

Until Sebastian.

Thinking about Sebastian made me want to strip my clothes off and masturbate again. Almost made me want to have sex with Jens just to be having sex.

"Ah, well, I'm going out to Leeds with friends. Want to come?"

I did want to. It sounded like a fun diversion, and the last thing I really wanted to do, despite my protestations to Sebastian, was work. I was tired and facing down these last twelve days with a growing sense of dread that I might actually not be able to find the proof I needed. And the more I thought that, the more I wanted to stick my head in the sand.

But I had an appointment on Monday afternoon with one of the staff at the Saint Bride Printing Library, and in the morning I had several calls to make to descendants of Anne Gracechurch, the ones I hadn't been able to reach previously or whose connection was slightly more obscure, who very likely didn't even know that their ancestor had been a fairly well-known author in her time.

He shrugged and left. I spent the day organizing myself for the week, and then working on the historical/cultural-context chapters of my dissertation. By seven in the evening, my creativity was sapped and my eyes were strained from staring at the computer. And I was hungry. The nuts, fruit, and cheese I'd snacked on throughout the day weren't going to cut it.

I stepped out into the living room. Neil, my other flatmate, was sitting on the futon sofa watching a rugby match, which was a regular occurrence. Both he and Jens had lived in the apartment months before I arrived, and apparently my room had belonged to a "chap" named Paul, who'd moved in with his girlfriend between terms.

The apartment looked like a bachelor pad and, aside

from clearing a space in the fridge and cleaning off the kitchen counters whenever I cooked, I hadn't made any effort to make it any less so.

I walked into the kitchen and opened the refrigerator. As I remembered, there was nearly nothing inside other than cheese, Neil's beer and a cardboard pizza box. I should have gone to the grocery store earlier since the one in the neighborhood closed at 5 p.m. on Sundays.

I was bored and hungry and had a stupid urge to call Sebastian. After all, if I wasn't going to work, why shouldn't I have some fun? Except, it was one night. Any more than that (even the fact that I *wanted* more than that) was a death wish. Dark Ages were officially over. I just had to stick to that.

I opened the freezer and magically found a frozen burrito I'd bought a few weeks earlier. There. Dinner found; problem solved. I could eat and push myself through a few more hours of work.

MONDAY STARTED GREAT. I made fabulous progress. If crossing people off of a list could be considered progress. But there was a lovely, middle-aged woman, Roberta Small, who was fascinated to learn about her ancestor, Anne Gracechurch, and who then assured me the only heirloom item she had was some silver plate from her paternal grandmother (who was from Spain). But she offered to call all of her relatives on her mother's side and see if anyone knew anything or had any old family records.

Then there was another branch of descendants, of whom Mrs. Small had never heard. Bruce Mallard, the eighty-eight-year-old (which I knew from his birth records) who I managed to get on the phone, turned out to be the "patriarch," so to speak, of his particular branch. He scanned through the family Bible to confirm that he was indeed related to an Anne Gracechurch, and then he revealed that he did in fact have a whole room filled with boxes and trunks and antiques that had been passed down through the family for generations. I was welcome to come sift through them all, and I made an appointment to come out to his house an hour outside of London by train the next day. The thought of a possible treasure trove buoyed me throughout the rest of the day, even when the "find" the archivist at the printing library had called me about turned out to be a rather underwhelming list of the books and pamphlets Anne's printer had published in the years 1809–1829. Underwhelming because, while Mead's name was mentioned there in '29, the list included no identifiers of any of the authors other than their names.

At seven thirty, I'd just flopped down on my bed to map out the best route to Luton when my phone rang. I recognized the number even though I'd only ever seen it before once, the day I'd programmed it into my phone at the National Archives' cafe. Despite myself, I was grinning, pleased.

"Sebastian," I said into the speaker. "You may have just gotten off work, but I have not."

"That's too bad. You must not be using your time efficiently during the day." His voice dripped over me, the way it had when I'd recognized it at the archives. The way it had during all the conversations we'd ever had.

"Because you want to sleep with me again."

"Sleep has nothing to do with it."

"Hah." If he was really calling me for help with his genealogy project, I'd be seriously annoyed. "I'm sure you can sift through the public records as well as I can. Isn't sifting through data your job?"

"Hah, and no, I didn't call for that either."

A shiver went through me at the import of his words. Good. He wanted what I wanted. The only difference was, I had a reason to say no.

"I didn't really have a chance to take you to dinner on Saturday. I doubt you've seen the best of London."

I thought of Sebastian in his expensive, tailored suit, which he could afford because he had an excellent job while I was still living the life of an impoverished student. I didn't know all that much about his background, but I knew that his family was well-off, and, even if he lived a fairly low-key life, he knew half the people whose faces littered the tabloids. Likely he did know the best restaurants and the best of everything. Very different from my frozen burrito of the night before. Which, thanks to my dwindling bank account and lack of credit, would be similar to what I would eat for the next two weeks.

I looked down at my computer. I'd made progress and Tuesday could easily be *the* day I'd been waiting for. Why not celebrate a bit?

Because that wasn't part of the plan. Speaking to him

again wasn't part of the plan. And . . . because it might be dangerous, might upset the delicate balance of my life.

"All right." I heard my voice like it was some other person's and the sound of it scared me. Was I sabotaging myself?

"I'll pick you up in thirty. Dress up."

He was off the phone before I'd even gathered my thoughts and registered his last words. Then I laughed, pushing the fear aside. That he felt he had to tell me to dress up made it clear he only knew the studious me, not the party girl who had been unleashed in his absence.

Not that I had brought much of my party attire with me to London, but I did have a few things, and as I changed into a slinky dress that showed off my legs, I was very glad I had.

I'd never been particularly overweight, but I'd slimmed down in the last two years. Right then, I was quite pleased with how I looked.

For the first time in four months, I broke out the makeup bag and set to work.

Neither of my flatmates was in the living room when I walked through, for which I was grateful. I didn't want to have to answer any questions about this particular booty call.

As he had said when he called three minutes earlier, Sebastian hadn't been able to find a parking spot and was waiting in his car downstairs. I opened the passenger-side door and slipped in.

His eyes slid over me appreciatively, and I felt that look in every part of my body. He had this way of being that was infinitely sexy, and he'd dressed up, too, in slacks and a jacket that could very well have been tailored to his body.

He leaned toward me, snaked one arm up until his hand curved around my neck. He drew me close, his mouth closing over mine. I twisted my body to lean into the drugging kiss.

"Good evening, Mina Cavallari."

"Good evening," I whispered. "Skipping your evening workout for me?" I imagined his body beneath those clothes—long, lean...

He gave me a look and I flushed, the subtext ridiculously clear.

"Good point," I said with a shaky laugh. "So, where are we heading?"

"Vaden Pierce's new place." The name meant nothing to me but I was thinking famous chef or restaurateur. At my blank expression, Sebastian elaborated. "He's Michelin starred. I haven't been to Ziva, but I have been to his other restaurants."

That sounded fine by me. I wasn't particularly experimental in my eating habits, but most of that was due to income and convenience, not an unwillingness to try new things.

"Now," he said, "tell me about why you look so radiant, unless it's all due to knowing you'll be properly fucked tonight."

I laughed. He was this very odd mix of elegant, perceptive, and crude. Oddly, the crude didn't bother me the way it would have with other men. There was something about the way Sebastian wore his lasciviousness that spoke straight to my erogenous zones. Which was why I was sitting in his car, for what was essentially an extended one-night stand.

As we drove through Brixton and Lambeth and back over the bridge past King's College, I told him about the progress I'd made, about my hopes for the Mallard collection.

He asked all the right questions, said all the right things, and I was starting to wonder what his family and school life had been like as a child because no one was this well trained to listen attentively. He was almost impossibly perfect. Except, considering the night he propositioned me to join him and Tanya, clearly he wasn't. No one was.

The restaurant was in the heart of Mayfair, and we parked at a car park before walking the short distance from there to Ziva. We descended to a windowless basement, and with the opulent decor, it was easy to forget that our table for two existed in any real world. Instead, as seemed to be usual for the time I was with Sebastian, we were on an island, focused solely on each other. Or at least, I focused solely on him.

"So what do you do when you aren't at work, or working out, or having sex?"

His lips curved up at the end of my question. I'd thrown that last in there to be as casually crude as he, but even saying it had felt a bit daring.

"My obsessions change," he said. I thought the answer, the choice of words, interesting. "Right now, it's you."

His gaze was searingly intense and I practically melted into my chair. He was good. What would have happened if I'd seen this side of him before? If he'd turned this focused attention on me earlier that year and the whole fiasco with Tanya had never happened? I had a slight suspicion that I might have been overwhelmed and unequal to it.

I was certainly still a bit overwhelmed but definitely not unequal. For good or for bad.

All the food at Ziva seemed designed to act as aphrodisiacs, and between the intensity of the flavors, the potency of the wine, and every glance Sebastian sent my way, I was more than ready to go back to his place.

Clearly, Sebastian felt the same way because the instant we entered his flat, before the door even fully shut closed, he was on me.

Dinner and the car ride home, all of that, was foreplay. There, against the wall of the entry hall, he pushed up my dress, pulled off my thong, slid a condom on, and then was inside me. With my legs wrapped around his hips, I met his open mouth with my own, loving the way each thrust slammed me back, the way his desire overpowered me completely.

There was something about this, about being taken so uninhibitedly, that turned me on more than anything else. I came in a shuddering, mewling rush, squeezing him with my thighs and my hands.

"That's it," he muttered, and then groaned, pushing up into me hard and relentlessly with his own orgasm.

We stood there for a moment, intertwined and gasping, sticky with exertion where we were joined.

Taking deep breaths, he pulled out, let me slide down to stand on my feet. His hair was messy and his face flushed, but he grinned down at me, and I grinned back with an answering sense of mischievous pleasure. "There, we took the edge off," he said. "Now let's get into the bedroom and do it properly."

MORNING CAME ALL too soon. Between the alarm he had set for work and the one I had set on my phone, the bedroom was a ringing mess of irritation. His bed was warm and comfortable. Even better, he was in it, and his naked body, which had brought me pleasure until the wee hours of the morning, was wrapped around mine.

He slipped out of bed first. I made a sound of protest even though I knew it was time to go. But it was a bit harder than it had been Sunday morning. I'd been spoiling my body, and the thought of not sleeping with him again was slightly upsetting, an empty, anxious feeling, like when an ice-cream store is out of the one flavor you crossed town to get.

That feeling made me even more anxious, propelling me back into doubt about my actions.

But I didn't have time for those sorts of thoughts. I needed to get to work.

"After I shower and dress, I'll drive you back to your flat."

I flipped the covers off me, hoping the cool air would

clear my mind and encourage me to actually leave the bed. Of course, the way he looked at me as I stretched my naked body gave me exactly the opposite idea.

"I'll take the Tube back," I said dismissively out of some latent sense of self-preservation. It was ridiculously stupid how easily he could affect me with just his eyes.

He picked up my dress from the floor and looked at it, then me, with one brow raised in question. "Are you certain?"

The walk of shame. Done many a time by students across the world, myself included. Oh God, how many times I'd done it in the past two years. The thought sickened me slightly. I shook my head to clear my mind. Did it really matter who stared at me as I navigated the steep staircases and escalators of the underground in my three-inch heels?

"You don't drive to work every day, do you?" After all these months, I knew a little about London. Generally speaking, like Boston, where I'd spent my undergrad years, if you could take public transportation somewhere, you did.

"No," he said, climbing back on the bed and looming over me. "But I also don't have a beautiful woman in my bed every day."

I laughed, partly because I knew if he didn't, he surely could, partly because he'd called me beautiful and partly because he could be such a gentleman. I moved my legs apart and his hips fell between, his hardening penis pressed against me. He made a small sound of pleasure and then lowered his head to lick my neck.

"If we had even thirty more minutes to spare, I know exactly what I'd do with this body of yours."

Show me, I wanted to say, despite the fact that I had a 10 A.M. appointment an hour outside London. That I still needed to get back to my apartment, change, and grab my backpack.

"Even five more minutes," he said, his voice almost a growl against my ear and his body pressed so firmly against mine that with just the slightest movement he'd be inside me. Which I wanted with sudden desperation.

It was a good thing we didn't have five more minutes. I was losing my sanity. Becoming completely obsessed with sex. Sex with Sebastian.

"But I'll just have to wait for tonight."

"Tonight?" The very word sounded dangerous.

"After I take you out for your celebratory dinner. After you find your missing link." With his optimistic words echoing how I felt, his suggestion seemed like a wonderful idea. Was there really anything wrong with extending a one-night stand into a three-night stand?

Yes. The answer was instant and weighty, but I pushed that doubt away. Leapt forward. Or maybe I was leaping to the side, far off track.

"All right," I said, despite my more dire thoughts, wrapping my legs around him riskily, considering he wasn't wearing the all-important barrier of a condom. "But I want you to know I have very high standards. I expect absolute pleasure."

Chapter Five

BRUCE MALLARD LIVED out in Luton, or rather in Leagrave, which apparently had once been its own village before becoming a suburb. It was about an hour from King's Cross by train. Of course, even passing through the King's Cross Station made me think of Sebastian and his apartment nearby, which would be empty at this hour since it was the workweek. After a good fifteen minutes daydreaming about sex, I forced myself to open my laptop and at least pretend to scan the notes I had about Anne's life.

I arrived at the Leagrave station just after ten in the morning and found a cab to drive me out to his house.

While I knew he didn't live in some Gracechurch ancestral home, as Anne had grown up in central Bedfordshire some distance away, I still didn't expect the little one-story midtwentieth-century bungalow that stood unprepossessingly in the middle of an unattractive residential neighborhood.

Bruce Mallard, however, was exactly what I had imagined the eighty-eight-year-old to be. Pale skin with rosy cheeks, thinning cotton-candy-like white hair. Hardy and in apparently good health but content with aging.

He shook my hand and welcomed me in, asking me instantly if I wanted any tea. He added that his wife had gone to visit their grandchildren down the road but would be home soon.

Even though I was antsy to see his stash, I sat down in the front parlor while he put tea on. Photographs and memorabilia decorated the room.

I stood up to look closer at one of the photographs that I thought must have been of Mallard when he was in his twenties.

"That was just after the war," he said, and I turned to see him crossing toward me. He pointed to another photograph. "That's my Sally."

I peered at the black-and-white image of a woman in a dress that had molded against her hip and leg in the wind, her dark hair smoothly coiffed despite that wind. So different from my ponytail and jeans.

"It's a lovely photograph."

"Yes." He paused a moment. "Sit. Tell me about this project." He referred to my dissertation as if it were some elementary-school assignment, as if maybe I'd be making a diorama or something.

"Your ancestor, Anne Gracechurch, was a fairly popular author during her time. But like many popular female authors of the day, and unlike the Brontës or Shelley, she faded into obscurity." I filled him in on what I had learned so far, about her friends and her life, clarifying the story for myself once more as I did. I could talk about this subject for hours, but of course, what I could learn from him was more relevant.

He stopped me briefly so he could get the tea: simple English Breakfast in little premade bags.

"So I'm hoping that you might have some items that belonged to her. I've been contacting all the other branches of her descendants." I mentioned Roberta Small and, whereas he hadn't been quite as interested in the older history, Mallard's eyes brightened at hearing about his distant relatives. He wanted to know at exactly what fork in the tree they diverged and determined to make contact with her.

We finished tea and, finally, he led me to a little addition in the rear of the property that was used as a storage room and at first glance appeared to be a treasure trove of antiques and family history. For a moment I felt like I was on one of the television shows in which an antiques dealer tells the homeowner what everything is worth. Then I focused. As cool as all of this old stuff was, vases, sideboards, silver plate, and other furnishings would not enlighten me as to anything about Anne Gracechurch. But even my untrained eye spotted the neoclassical chair with its frayed and rotting seat cushion. Maybe he *had* kept papers and correspondence from the first half of the nineteenth century.

"Why do you keep it all?" I asked, navigating my

way through narrow and sometimes nonexistent aisles. "Clearly most of this furniture is of no use to you."

He shrugged. "Sally wanted everything new but, maybe someday one of the kids wants a bit of our history. When I die, they can decide what they want to do with it all." He led me to a trunk in the corner. "You might want to start here." He unearthed two chairs that were in relatively good shape and sat down. I knelt on the floor at first as I opened the trunk, which itself, judging from the Art Nouveau motifs etched into the cracked leather, was at least a hundred years old.

Excitement thrummed through me as I pushed the lid up. The stacks of loose papers and leather-bound books nearly had me doing cartwheels (which I can't actually do very well). Something of value would be in here, surely.

Two hours later, after a brief break to meet Sally, and after Bruce had long since decided he didn't need to watch over me, I'd made it through two-thirds of the first trunk, which was filled with ledgers and correspondence, none of which were older than 1914.

Four hours after that, with one more brief break to eat the very lovely and generous luncheon Sally prepared, I'd made it through two more trunks, one of which was crammed with moth-eaten linens and another with more ledgers and correspondence, and I was elbows deep in a third. Already, I'd set aside one promising book of household accounts and a packet of letters that actually were addressed to Anne. By the date on the first, I had hopes that it was the same Anne. Currently fascinating me were photo albums that went back in time to the nineteenth century. So far, the oldest I'd found dated from 1886, twenty-five years after Anne Gracechurch had passed away, but there were still three more inches of depth to riffle through.

Which were mostly filled with a random assortment of color photographs from the late twentieth century. Whoever had last packed away this box had not attempted to do so chronologically.

Another layer down, wrapped in tissue, I found what I was pretty sure was a daguerreotype. And on the back, it said Reginald and Anne 1857. I flipped it around to stare at the semidecomposed image of what I thought to be a husband and wife. Not just any husband and wife.

I took out my phone, quickly snapped several photos of the front and back, and e-mailed them off to my advisor. Regardless of anything else, *this* was a definite find. I'd never before seen so much as a portrait of Anne, and in front of me was an image of the woman in whose life I'd become immersed.

She looked matronly and stern in the picture. In fact, they both looked overly serious, but I knew that was likely due to having to stand still for a longer period of time than necessary for our modern instant snapshots. She would also have been about sixty-one when it was taken. I tried to imagine her daily life based on this photo and the letters of hers I had already read. Her voice had always been humorously observant.

My chest ached as I gently wrapped the photograph back in its tissue paper. I didn't know much about preservation, but I'd have to find out immediately.

I riffled through the rest of the trunk quickly and, finding nothing else of immediate interest, placed everything but the daguerreotype back.

Then, all of the trunks in the addition having been sorted through, I turned my attention to the packet of letters that I had previously set aside, and untied the twine that bound them. The first letter was from a Mrs. Howell. I opened my backpack and pulled out my laptop. Luckily, there was still some charge. I clicked on the "character" list I had created for Anne's life, searched for "Howell," and found the name of a second cousin. Interesting, but how close a confidante was this Mrs. Howell?

I turned my attention back to the letter. I'd grown comfortable decoding the slanted script of many nineteenth-century correspondents and within two lines realized this was a dull recitation of domestic life. Like, what little Henry was up to and how Mr. Howell's ague fared. Mrs. Howell did not have nearly the way with words of her cousin. I scanned the rest of the letter quickly, looking for anything that jumped out as interesting. A reference to Anne's visit six months earlier required a notation in my files, but other than that, nothing.

Three more letters from Sarah Howell, with more about her son and her husband. Then a letter from another cousin, Gordon Albany (Albany being Anne's maiden name). There, at least, was a reference to her novels—although somewhat scathing—with a lecture on why she should refrain from putting any more into print. I took a photograph of the letter and then typed the pertinent text into my notes. It gave interesting context for Anne's life and the reception of her work yet still provided no connection between Anne and James Mead.

Nor did any of the other letters, which continued in the same vein: all from family members, some mentioning her books, some only domestic matters, and some both. I was very curious as to how Anne had responded to these, but simply thinking about the task of attempting to track down possibly already discarded letters overwhelmed me.

I placed the stack of letters next to the daguerreotype with the intention of getting them copied or scanned at some point, and picked up the Gracechurch household accounts from the year 1856. Why had this particular volume been saved when so many others appeared to have been discarded? Or if not discarded, kept elsewhere?

I flipped open to the first page. Studied it. Tried to get a sense of its rhythm. I wasn't entirely certain what I was looking for, maybe a notation of income earned from the publisher or anything of that nature. After all, she had published her second to last novel in 1855. Instead, what greeted me were grocery items, butcher bills, coal for heating, and more of the day-to-day expenses necessary for keeping a midnineteenth-century home. I kept turning pages, one after the other, until finally I reached the last.

While certainly Anne had earned money from her books, and supposedly that was her original impetus for writing, she didn't appear to keep track of that income here.

I left the Mallards' home with smiles, thanking them

for their time and generosity and with the promise to return in a week with the items I was borrowing. I was half-amazed they actually let me leave with them. With everything carefully packed away in my backpack, I slid into a taxi and headed for the station.

But the minute the taxi pulled away, my smile was gone. If my goal were only to learn more about Anne Gracechurch and her life, then the day was a success. But my intention was not to be simply her biographer or historian but to extend my discussion of her work with a critical analysis of her choice to adopt an alter ego.

This had been a true treasure trove, yet I'd found nothing! How likely was it that I'd find another such stash of previously undisturbed artifacts? Not very likely at all.

Especially with only ten more days left in England.

I tried to put the disappointment from my mind and focus on the positives, but I heard that ticktock of the figurative clock clearly in my mind.

Ten more days.

I boarded the train back to London and pulled out my spiral notebook. Even though I had numerous such lists already, I started writing down all the leads that were left to me and any that the day's jaunt might have opened up. There was a desperate comfort in the process. Methodical. A list to check off.

Halfway back to London I remembered my "celebratory" date with Sebastian. I fished out my phone to call him, then stared at it, the time glaring back at me. Just after seven. He'd said he'd call as soon as he was off from work, which meant he wasn't off yet. Which meant I had time to think.

I wanted to cancel. By no means did I feel celebratory. Yet, why cancel? Every way I looked, I was finding dead ends. In the next ten days, it was unlikely anything spectacular would turn up. Why shouldn't I at least have some hot sex?

I refused to answer my own question. There were too many reasons why I should call him and cancel. But I was deliberately not thinking.

Forty minutes later, in the cramped little bathroom of my shared flat, I stood under the tepid water, with its intermediate short bursts of hot and then freezing-cold water. What was it about water that made the tears come so easily? I reached a hand out against the tile and bent my head down.

I thought I was so in control, so able to handle everything, and yet, here I was, failing.

But it was stupid to be crying and self-pitying. Nothing ever got done that way. I took a deep breath and finished washing the conditioner out of my hair. By the time I stepped out of the shower, it was 8:30 P.M. and he still hadn't called. He'd said sometimes he worked long hours, but now I was getting antsy. And hungry. The very least he could do was call to let me know about what time it would be. Or he could cancel.

Finally, I picked up my phone. Then nearly dropped it as it rang loudly. Okay, then.

"It's Seb."

"I know," I said with a laugh. "I was about to call you."

"I'm sorry about how late it is. Have you eaten yet?" He sounded exhausted, which didn't bode well for a night of decadent, take-my-mind-off-my-problems sex.

"No." But what I really needed to say was, *Don't bother coming. It's been fun, but it's over.*

Yet I couldn't. I *wanted* to see him.

"I know I promised you a celebratory meal"—I winced—"but how do you feel about takeaway? There's good Vietnamese just around the corner from my office."

"Actually, that's fine."

"Great. I'll be there in thirty."

The short, abrupt conversation left me feeling even more unsettled and despondent. While I hadn't felt particularly celebratory, somehow we'd gone from Sebastian wining and dining me at the fanciest of restaurants to eating takeout in my apartment. With my flatmates watching television in the living room.

Not particularly conducive to romance. Or to sex.

Somewhat irritated, I grabbed my laptop and moved to the small, round dining table that bordered the living room.

"She's alive," Neil said in a stage whisper to Jens. He gave me a big wink.

"Not only am I alive, but I have company coming over in half an hour," I said. I'd never had brothers, but I'd gotten used to Neil's teasing in the last few months.

That got Jens's attention, and he twisted his body toward me, resting his arm on the back of the couch. "The friend you were with the other night?"

"The same." I stared at the television beyond them. It

was some reality TV show that I'd never seen before.

"I was going to meet friends at the pub, but I think I'll hang about a bit more."

I laughed. Of course Jens would want to see who the guy was who had actually gotten into my pants when he'd had no such luck. I flipped open my laptop and tuned him and the television out. I was only out here to make sure I heard Sebastian when he arrived and to avoid any overly awkward conversation.

But with all my research documents already open and staring me in the face, my momentary diversion fled. Ten days. One of which was a Sunday. There were still many avenues left to me, but they were all the slimmest chances and the most difficult to pursue, or ones that had only popped up in the last two weeks.

But some of this work I could do from the States. And, if necessary, I could likely return as soon as next summer. Or if I worked and saved up more money again, I could come back as early as the spring. Not ideal. Possibly, it wouldn't even be worth coming back. Maybe I'd never find the link I was hoping for.

I checked my e-mail. There was one from my advisor with multiple exclamation points. She clearly thought the photograph a fabulous find. But then, she also was the one who had pushed for me to have a less ambitious backup argument, and the photograph made that backup thesis slightly more exciting for her.

Why did a reasonable, rational thing like having to resort to a plan B make me feel like a failure?

But I knew why. It was because I'd failed when I

missed the deadlines for my fellowship. I'd failed when I'd let one stupid interaction—one guy—affect my life in such a huge way.

The doorbell buzzed. Two pairs of male eyes and knowing smiles turned my way. I rolled my eyes as I stood to answer the door. They could be a bit less obvious.

I opened the door. As soon as I saw Sebastian standing there in his suit and tie, a slim messenger bag slung over his arm and a brown bag of fragrant food in his right hand, nothing else mattered but the heat that washed over me and the strange, sudden joy at seeing him again.

My attraction to Sebastian had been half as great back in New Jersey, mostly because, while I hadn't been a virgin, I'd known nearly nothing about sex. Good sex, that is. Knowledge made every anticipatory sensation within me sharper.

"Hi," I said, almost shyly. He had shadows under his eyes, looked like he'd had a long day. I knew our late night the previous day must not have helped, yet his lips curved up in a sensual promise.

Desire surged inside me and heat gathered between my legs. I had it bad. *It* being a serious case of lust.

"Can I come in?"

I laughed self-consciously and stepped aside, only then, as I closed the door and turned, remembering our audience. I stepped forward for introductions but was too late. Sebastian was already saying hello with an outstretched hand. Introducing himself as an old university friend of mine.

Friend. We *had* been friends at one point. Now we

were lovers, but I wasn't entirely certain about the friendship aspect, no matter what I had said to Neil and Jens earlier.

Sebastian made some comment about the show they were watching, and I realized that it had changed from the reality show to the finale of one of those next big popstar competitions. I slid the brown bag from his grasp and took it into the kitchen.

I should never have worried about awkwardness. Apparently Sebastian knew how to take charge of any situation with a smooth, natural charm. He was the antithesis of what anyone in an American high school would have imagined a math major to be. Had he always been this way? Or had he simply grown up and developed that ease over time?

In contrast, I was a complete introvert. Well, perhaps not completely considering the last two years, but for the majority of my life, my impulse had been to avoid people in preference for my books and studies. It had always been easier. At least, until the day after Sebastian's graduation.

I cleared space on the counter and pulled out all the little paper boxes and plastic containers. There was soup (pho, I gathered), spring rolls, and then some rice and another dish that looked like chicken. It was way more food than two people could eat. I pulled two bowls and plates down from the cupboard and set them out with utensils.

"I wasn't certain what you'd like," Sebastian said quietly as he came up behind me and wrapped his arms around me. I melted back against him, my hand still clutching a fork. He kissed me on the temple, and then on my neck, before letting go and reaching for a plate. "God, I'm starving."

"It all looks good," I said, watching him as he served himself. He was just so comfortable in his skin. As at home here as he was at his own place. But now that he was no longer touching me, I could see that hint of exhaustion at the corner of his eyes.

"How was work?" I asked.

"Ah, the usual. Started a new project for a new client. How was your stop in Luton?"

"I . . ." I stopped myself before I said anything negative. Instead, I took a moment to focus on serving myself food as well. Sebastian hadn't chosen to get too deep into the details of his own work. Likely, I shouldn't prose on and on about my own either. "Fascinating. Ultimately not what I hoped, but definitely worth the trip out. Can I get you something to drink? Actually, there's not much here. A glass of water?"

"Water is fine," he said with a grin, then reached for my plate.

A few moments later I joined him at the table in the living room and placed our glasses down.

We ate in silence, having each brushed over our day's work, and really, what else was there to talk about? In front of us, on the television, some seventeen-year-old singer who had just been voted off the show was watching a retrospective of her performances.

I wanted to say something about how I really felt, but Neil and Jens were several feet away. Beyond which, the knowledge that I'd be leaving soon and it didn't really matter if Sebastian understood my deep emotional needs or my disturbed psyche kept me silent as I ate.

"Do you watch this show?" I asked finally, feeling ridiculously self-conscious of the silence, of how Neil and Jens might judge it.

He laughed. "No. But one of the receptionists at work is avid about it. I think she wants to try out next season."

"What shows *do* you like to watch?" I couldn't remember us ever talking about television before. Music, yes. Especially when once he'd pulled out his phone to identify a song playing on the coffee shop's radio. How crazy that I remembered that little moment? That I remembered all of those moments.

"I don't really watch much on the telly at all."

"So you just work, work out, eat, and sleep?"

"And fuck," he added in a much quieter voice, his gaze full of promise. "Don't forget that."

As if my body would let me forget the sex part of it all. At least we had that. Since I didn't need or want more from Sebastian Graham, and sex was clearly his forte, it was all good.

"Maybe we should skip ahead," I suggested, putting my spoon down.

The edge of his lip quirked up. "Excellent idea."

I stacked up our plates and took them back to the kitchen. Sebastian followed me and, without saying anything, closed up the leftover food and placed it in the fridge. Perhaps not much of a celebratory dinner, but at least I'd have leftovers.

Then he had me in his arms and his lips were on mine. Domesticity gave way to charged desire.

"Where's your room?"

I led him back across the apartment, avoiding looking at either of my flatmates. When we were safely in my room, door shut, I practically threw myself at him.

It was so nice not to think about the time running down on my trip or my failure to do what I'd set out to do. I lost myself in his mouth, his touch, the way that, in lifting up on my toes to press myself flat against him, I was subsumed by his existence.

His hands were already under my skirt, rounded over my backside, as he pulled me even closer, his erection hard against me.

"I cannot get enough of you," he muttered. The words thrilled me in a primal way.

I reached up to loosen his tie, to start the process of releasing him from his work attire. Then I nearly fell as his fingers reached between my legs and stroked me over my panties. Apparently, I almost choked him, too, as his hands left me and he reached up to take over the business of the tie.

"Sorry." I stepped back and watched him. I wasn't entirely certain what it was about seeing him with that tie loose about his neck that made me want to fall to my knees and take him in my mouth. I'd never felt this obsessed with sex and a man's body before. At the same time that I reveled in it, it frightened me.

Made me wonder who I was.

As he pulled the tie over his head, I stepped away, wanting distance to clear my head. I was using him the way people used alcohol or other substances—to escape the reality of my life. Was that so bad?

"Don't go too far away," he said, reaching for me. But I stepped out of range again, not that the room was all that big. In fact, the frame of the single bed pressed against my calves.

"I don't think I'm going to find the link," I blurted out. When his hands fell to his sides, and he looked at me confused—whether by the abrupt change of topic or by wondering what the hell I was talking about, I didn't know—I elaborated, "Between Anne Gracechurch and James Mead. I found this fabulous photograph of her. No one's ever even found a painting of her let alone a daguerreotype before. My advisor is beyond excited."

"But you're not."

I shook my head. Talking felt as unreal as having sex with him did. Like it wasn't totally me, and yet, I just kept going.

"I have ten days left here, and despite all the work I've done, and I have been relentless," I said with no false modesty because until bumping into Sebastian at the archives, I had been completely focused on my work. "Despite that, I'm going to be leaving here with nothing to show for it. With my thesis resting merely on forensic analysis, which, interesting as it might be as a starting point, doesn't give me a slam-dunk-fabulous entry into the world of academia."

"And that's your plan? After this, back to uni, finish up your dissertation, and start the search for a faculty position?"

"That's the plan," I said slowly, but I couldn't stop the hot flush that filled my body, the sudden sensation of distress. I blinked. Looked down and away, trying to compose myself.

"Mina . . . ?" Maybe it was how late it was, or the gentleness of his tone. Maybe it was the early excitement of the day and then the letdown. Or it could have simply been being tired of hiding my shame, the embarrassment of failure, from everyone. All I know is that the floodgates fell open and tears were running down my face.

I looked away, wiping at my eyes with the back of my hands, and heard the door to my bedroom open and close. I looked back, and stared at the space where he had been. Some experiment in empowerment. I was a mess and this was a disaster.

More tears dripped down my cheeks and self-disgust filled me. I had to get myself together. I had to—

The door opened. He was back and holding out a wad of napkins from the Vietnamese takeaway.

"Thanks," I muttered, taking two. He placed the rest on the desk.

We stood there in silence a minute more, until the only remnant of my tears was the blotchiness of my skin and red-rimmed eyes.

"This . . . isn't just about today."

I blinked in surprise.

"The Mina I know can handle some setbacks. Knows how to put them in perspective."

The Mina he knows. Despite my depression, I wanted to laugh.

Instead, I sat down heavily on the bed. He sat down next to me, shrugging out of his jacket. This wasn't my life. This was some other place, other time, as if I were living in a dreamworld.

Except, this *was* my life.

"I'm sorry," I started, shifting until I was cross-legged and facing him. "I just . . . It's been a hard year."

Yet it was hard because I'd spent the previous year fucking around, literally and figuratively, and I'd had to deal with the consequences. Had to take a hard look at myself and who I'd become.

Apparently, someone who still would jump into bed with a near stranger on the first night. Not that there was necessarily anything wrong with that, as long as it wasn't taking away from my professional goals.

He was watching me, expressionless. Just listening.

"I missed some important deadlines." I saw his eyes widen ever so slightly, surprised. Yeah, that sort of behavior wouldn't fit his previous conception of studious, obsessive Mina. "I didn't get the fellowship I needed." My lips twisted as I shrugged. He didn't need to know why all this had happened. It was just too embarrassing really. Because then we'd actually have to talk about *that night* and the lasting effect it had had on my life. I really didn't need Sebastian thinking I was more of a freak than he likely already did, or that I was some obsessed girl who had stalked him here in London. "So I've been working, saving up money for this trip."

"You made things harder on yourself but . . . you're here." He was still watching me carefully, as if he knew there was more to this.

"I know, but it's embarrassing." I looked down. "I haven't told anyone. Not my parents, or my friends. Well, Sophie. I guess I told Sophie."

Sophie, my oldest friend, who I'd met in seventh grade, who I still hadn't talked to since I'd accidentally called her too early on Sunday morning. Despite different colleges and different life paths, we'd stayed in touch. *She* had her shit together. A job in New York City, a boyfriend, a life.

The way Sebastian clearly had his life worked out. He could apparently have threesomes, one-night stands, weeklong flings with old university acquaintances . . . all with no detrimental effect on his career. Why was I the only idiot who couldn't balance it all?

"What happened?"

I shook my head, my lips pressed tightly together. "It doesn't matter. I was stupid and lost focus." Then I laughed, trying to brush it all off, to give some satisfying version of the truth. "You know, I was always the straight-A, study-round-the-clock type. Never gave my parents trouble. Had goals and achieved them. Maybe I needed a break."

"Understandable," he said. "I always admired your intensity. But all work and no play . . ." He smiled. There was a touch of something lascivious in that smile, like he wanted me to think of the night before, and of that morning. I was hot at the mere suggestion, willing to strip and spend the rest of the night in bed if he made the slightest move. Then he turned serious again. "And clearly you're ready to work. Is being an English professor still what you want to do?"

He'd put his finger right on another question that had been dogging me the last few months. He was perceptive. In the two years since I'd last seen him, I'd forgotten there was anything more to him than a rude perv.

But Sebastian Graham was actually nice. Which was ... unsettling.

"I don't know," I admitted. "But I can't live with the failure of not finishing and not following this through."

"Gracechurch or the PhD?"

I shrugged. It was nearly the same thing. Finish the research and dissertation. Or something like that.

"At this point, while I almost definitely can do the second, I'm no longer confident about the first."

"You don't think you can find what you need?"

"I've run out of time."

"You have to go back next week?" He kept asking questions, relentlessly, as if he were leading toward a solution. It was such a male thing to do and it irritated me. If he wanted to listen, that was one thing, but there wasn't any solution to this.

"Seb, stop. I'm out of money. Maybe I'll be able to come back next spring or summer, but who knows. Maybe that would be a waste."

"But if you could afford it, you'd stay longer?"

I rolled my eyes.

He grinned. I had no idea he could be so irritating. It was better if we just stuck to sex.

"What if I hired you?" My eyebrows rose. "To help me with research. The archivists charge on average £40 an hour." Oh. With his genealogy project.

Then it hit me. Wow. He was offering to pay me. I stared at him in semidisbelief, my lips curved half up as if I wanted to be ready to laugh in case this was a joke. Or laugh if it wasn't a joke.

"I'm absolutely serious. I could use the help, Mina, and you could stay the summer."

I didn't even know if my room was available past next week, but forty an hour could quickly add up. Except, how weird would that be, to take a job from Sebastian?

"I'm on an academic visitor visa. I'm not allowed to work for money."

"Like anyone would know," he said with a shrug. "Better yet, you could stay at my place, for the summer." When I didn't answer, he continued, "I can't offer a private room, but by now you know it's far more hospitable than this grotty flat."

I stared at him like he'd sprouted an extra head. We'd had sex. Been having sex for less than a week, and he was asking me to move in with him. It sounded like a horrible idea. One doomed for misery. Yet . . . part of me wanted to say yes, regardless of my research and how much time I'd have to finish it. Wanted to say yes because he was a guy I'd had a crush on and was wildly attracted to. Because it was like playing house. Sharing his bed every night, having sex like we'd had–I'd lose myself there. It sounded wonderful, like an actual relationship, like something the old Mina would have wanted.

If I said yes, this wasn't just extending a one-night stand out a few days. This was . . . potentially complicated.

"*Not* that I'd expect a repeat performance, although I'm not against it." There was a definite teasing note in his voice to match that grin. "You'll have the place to yourself most of the day."

But if I didn't sleep with him again . . .

Of course I wanted to. Some secret part of me that I couldn't honestly deny counted that as a perk. An hour or two of sex at night would hardly take away from my daytime research. I wasn't some athlete needing to direct all that sexual energy toward the game.

He was offering me the chance to finish without having to go back to the US, apply for grants or save up funds, then wait until next summer to come back.

"That's very generous of you."

"Not generous." He smiled that quirky, devastating smile again. "Self-serving. Taking advantage of an opportunity. Adapting to failure."

I laughed. "To *my* failure, you mean."

"No, to mine." He moved closer to me. He was just so overwhelming, so overtly sexual, liquid sensuality. "I want to know what happened to this club but, that day at the archives, the only thing I managed to do well was run into you. And, as for that, I should have found you in January."

He played with the strap of my tank top, running his fingers under it, over my skin.

"I would have had four more months to fuck you every which way."

His words were blunt, rather vulgar really, and they hit me hard in the gut and between my legs. While the first night he'd been gentlemanly and attentive in his approach to sex, I was learning he had more of an edge to him. As if frequent sex turned on some latent dominant switch in his head.

His hands dropped, pulled on the waistband of my skirt, and slid it down over my hips. I didn't stop him. As the skirt dropped, so did he. To his knees in front of me.

"Legs apart," he ordered softly. Curious and aroused, I did as he said. Over the silky material of my panties, he cupped me with his hand, the pressure of his fingers making me all too aware of how damp I was. Through the fabric, his thumb swept over my clit. I sucked in my breath at the sensation. Which he followed with the wet heat of his mouth.

My knees nearly buckled and I reached forward desperately, grabbing at his shoulders for support.

If I'd had four months of this type of pleasure, I likely wouldn't have gotten any work done at all.

The filmy fabric that separated his tongue from my flesh was absolute torture. But then, when he slid the underwear down as well, when his mouth was on me with no barrier, I sighed at the sweetness of that first touch. Shuddered at the sharp pleasure of one finger parting me, entering me. Then another.

I looked about the room as if searching for something that would help me, would sustain me against too much pleasure. For a moment, I saw myself in that small single room that was cramped with research books and my luggage, half-dressed, with a man's mouth on me. Not just any man.

Sebastian.

Who had fueled my fantasies for two years. I looked down and watched his mouth cover me as if I were watching some porn video. The tide swept over me fast, unexpectedly, and I cried out, my knees buckling as my hips moved forward against him. He held me firm, but I drooped over him as he kissed me lightly where I pulsed.

He stood, caught my trembling body up in his arms, and laid me down on the bed, my hips at the edge.

"Staying?"

I let out a breathy laugh and watched him as he retrieved a condom from his back pocket, then unbuttoned his pants. He didn't undress any more, only pushed his boxers and trousers down, freeing his erection. "Do you have any idea how sexy you look right now? Spread open for me? Your pussy soft and wet. The taste of you still on my lips."

I didn't answer. Couldn't. I watched him roll the condom on, desperate for him to come closer. Then he did, parting me, pressing into me. He reached under my thighs and lifted my legs so that they rested against his chest. It wasn't a position that allowed me to do much of anything but enjoy the feel of him sliding in and out, slowly at first and then faster, until he was pounding against me, the slap of our sweaty bodies loud in the room, the fold of his trousers scraping against my skin.

Fuck me every which way. Like I was his little sex toy. A hole for him to fuck.

He slammed against me hard and stayed there, hands gripping tight at my hips, almost painfully. I watched him as he released himself inside me, eyes closed, head thrown slightly back, mouth open. A primal pleasure spiraled through me at being the generator of that look. Then he opened his eyes and looked down at me, slowly pulling out before thrusting back in yet again. Softer now, but shuddering at the lingering sensations.

He pulled out and, before I had a chance to think, was back between my legs, mouth hot on my clit, licking me like he was starving.

I came within seconds, shocked at the orgasm that had snuck up on me. But he kept his mouth on me, licking more slowly, lingeringly. Kissing me.

I blinked, the corners of my eyes damp.

Every which way.

Chapter Six

HE LEFT EARLY in the morning. I had a little more than one week left in the shared flat, but Sebastian was adamant that after work he'd come pick me up and we'd move my things. There was nice Sebastian, sexy Sebastian, ballsy Sebastian, ambitious Sebastian, and then this other version of him, that, once he'd determined my complicity, had no trouble ordering me about.

In my head, I readjusted the thematic relevance of our interactions. So it wasn't the full circle of a one-night stand; it was a tangent of that. This was Sebastian as solution, just as two years ago he had been the problem. The neatness of that significance comforted me. Made it easier to ignore the moral ambiguity of our agreement, the significance of the fluffy genealogy project for which I'd be well paid while sharing his bed and living in his apartment.

I spent the day settling things that needed to be

settled. Informed Neil that I was moving early (which naturally made me the recipient of some extremely suggestive jokes about my relationship with my "friend"), changed my airline ticket, cleaned up my room, and packed everything I could into the duffel bag and backpack with which I had arrived. The numerous papers and spiral notebooks I had acquired were stacked in a shopping bag.

I finished the Vietnamese food when I stopped for lunch, then searched for a good copying facility nearby where I could take the material I'd borrowed from Mr. Mallard. I found a place that specialized in archival copies and made an appointment for the following day.

I was exhausted, partially from lack of sleep and partially from the activity, and was shocked to see that it was still relatively early. I had two hours at least before Sebastian showed, and, considering the previous night, more likely four.

Finally, I took out my laptop and tried to focus on my work. But it was hard. I'd hit what felt like a massive dead end the day before. I had calls out with little hope of them being returned with positive news. I didn't want to do anything that had to do with my dissertation.

I wanted to fast-forward to Sebastian's flat and Sebastian's bed and not think.

But considering that train of thought was exactly the sort that would get me in trouble, I forced myself to make a list of all the veins of information I hadn't yet mined. I had more than two months instead of nine days. Additionally, I'd have some extra spending money when I helped Sebastian with his project. If I needed to travel outside of London for research in a week or two, I likely could.

Despite the negative outlook with which I had started work, several hours later, when my cell phone rang and projected Sebastian's name (he'd graduated from a recognized number to being an actual contact), I'd made progress and felt optimistic.

As I left that dingy little flat for the last time, I determined to also leave the negativity and weight of the past behind.

ON THE WAY to his apartment, we stopped for takeaway. He pulled into what would have been an alley back in the US but here was a labeled street, and then we waited as the gate to the underground parking garage of the huge modern apartment complex slid open. The garage descended three stories underground, each ramp shockingly steep. Sebastian had explained that first night that in London space was at a premium, and people tended to build down these days, even in a new complex that wasn't limited by historic preservation. We pulled into a narrow space, no SUVs here, then crossed the garage to the elevator. Sebastian insisted on carrying my duffel bag, slinging it over his shoulder as if he were the one backpacking through Europe.

Had he ever done that, or had his entire life been one of privilege and luxury?

Certainly, this apartment building, with its gleaming modern elevator accented with brushed steel, was a luxury.

Walking over the threshold of his apartment was oh-so-different from the last time. Though the buzz of sexual attraction and physical awareness still permeated the space between us, so did a sense of distance.

He placed my bag down in the living room and I hesitantly put my backpack next to it. I took a look around the room as if I hadn't just been there two days ago, walking naked from the bathroom to his bedroom.

His bedroom. Heat rushed through my body, and I slung a sidelong glance at him. *What now?*

"Make yourself at home," he said with a rather elegant little gesture that made me focus on his hands again. Long fingers. I clenched tightly inside at the simple memory of those fingers penetrating me. As if he had no idea what was going through this sex-crazed little brain of mine, he strode over to the sofa and lifted a cushion slightly.

"When you want it to be a sofa bed, there are clean sheets in the cupboard. I've never actually had anyone use it before."

Not that I would be using it either. But I nodded and smiled since, clearly, we were playing a polite game of pretend. We stood there a moment longer, the silence stretching.

"Thanks for letting me stay here," I said finally.

"There's not much in the fridge freezer," he said. "But feel free to take anything you want. And dishes are in the cupboards in all the usual spots."

He moved with purpose then, pulling out plates. I

opened the bag of food and arranged the containers on the table.

"Is this what you normally do for dinner?" I asked when he joined me.

He shook his head. "No. Well, I suppose in a way. I usually pick up something prepared at the market. A bit healthier."

He lived a classic bachelor life. Not so different from how I'd been living in that shared flat but very different from my life back in the States. I liked to cook. Had to, really, to save money. And since the easiest way to eat cheaply as a single person is to cook in bulk, that's what I normally did. My freezer was always stacked with food for the month.

"That's good."

We sat there in silence for a minute, each putting food on our plates. Chow mein and broccoli beef. This was first night of *living* with him, even if it would only be until partway through August. So strange, so domestic.

"So," I said finally. "Tell me about this project of yours."

"Right. Where to begin. When my grandfather, Viscount Stanton, died last year—" I blinked. *Viscount*? "—he left me his journals. Apparently my grandfather was far more verbose on paper than he ever was conversationally. He'd been keeping these journals, one for every year, since the age of six."

"How old was he when he passed away?"

"Ninety-three."

Eighty-seven journals. I shook my head at the thought. If only Anne Gracechurch had been as prolific.

"So I started reading them. Well, I skipped the first twelve years. He lived in a very different time. Inherited the title at twenty-four, in the middle of World War II."

My paternal grandparents had been in Italy during the war. Moved to the US in the fifties. I'd always been interested in their stories of wartime.

"He married a year later. Claimed he felt some pressure after his father's death to continue the line."

It seemed so old-fashioned, the stuff of the nineteenth century more than the twentieth, but then, the first decades of any century were often more an extension of the previous than some great cultural break.

"Where does this club fit in?" I asked.

"He belonged to it. At least, until it was destroyed during the bombings. Actually, he mentioned that only in passing as he'd stopped attending shortly before his wedding."

Even with the little Sebastian had said so far, I could see the romantic appeal of a club that disappeared in the tragedy of WWII.

"Where was it?"

"He didn't say. Nor did he say if it had been in the same location since its inception."

"But his father belonged. And his grandfather?"

"At least one Bosworth had belonged to Harridan House in each generation for the previous 150 years. The membership seems to have been a point of pride." He shook his head, a small, twisted smile on his lips.

"The club is named Harridan House?" It was a strange name for any club, but considering it was likely a bastion of masculinity, perhaps it simply wore its chauvinism on its sleeve.

"Yes, odd, I know," he said. "And the membership was entirely male although female guests were allowed and encouraged."

Suspicion tickled at the back of my neck. "Females encouraged is unusual. Was that in recent years? What was the purpose of the club?"

A full grin split Sebastian's face. "From my understanding, it was half brothel, half swingers club. Completely secretive and exclusive, and run by a woman known only as Madame Rouge."

I let out a disbelieving laugh. "Of course. I should have guessed that debauchery runs in your family."

"Yes, passed down like the Stanton Rubies," he said wryly.

"And your grandfather recognized that gene in you and left you his journals."

Sebastian looked down, the smile leaving his face. "No. I believe he left me those because he knew I'd be the only one to care."

At once, the club was less interesting than Seb's family history. I wanted to delve into it, to learn what made him who he was and what was beneath the charming, seductive exterior.

"Your father—"

"I haven't read all of his journals yet," Sebastian said, interrupting me. "I'm partway through the fifties. For the most part, my grandfather stopped mentioning Harridan House the year he married. Said his next visit would be his last. There was one more note the day the building was destroyed."

"And what do you want to know?"

"Everything. As much as we can discover from the day it was founded to the day it closed. What happened to it after WWII? What happened to its owner? Who was this Madame Rouge?"

It didn't seem an impossible task.

"I don't take holiday until August," Sebastian said, answering my unspoken question. There are limits to the resources available online, and I have only a handful of Saturdays to go to the archives. I can do it, yes, but you can do it faster and, likely, more thoroughly."

I nodded, slowly. Then laughed. Of course, it would be a sex club. Apparently, Sebastian's *obsessions* were all fairly related.

I put down my chopsticks and wiped my mouth with my napkin. Then I reached for my backpack and pulled out a notebook and pen. Despite the strangeness of the situation, if I was accepting money and shelter from him, it was essential I keep things as professional as possible. Time to get down to business.

I flipped to the last third of the notebook and jotted down the few details he had given. "So what have you done so far?"

"I'll e-mail it to you."

I put my pen down. Turned my attention back to the food even though I was well past full. I pushed the noodles around with my chopsticks and then finally placed them down again.

He took a final bite and then laid his down on his empty plate.

It was early. Not even eight in the evening. Tonight would likely set a pattern for the rest of our time together. I needed to unpack, find a place for my things. I just wasn't certain how this was all going to work.

"What about the journals? Are they here?"

"Yes. They take up a good portion of the linen cupboard."

Sebastian kept all eighty-seven journals in the closet. While he cleaned up the table and put leftover food away, I took journals 13–25 and stacked them on the coffee table to begin tackling tomorrow.

I turned around, found him standing there watching me. I wanted to know what he was thinking, but his face gave no hint.

"I'm going to work out."

"After eating? I thought you had to wait an hour?"

He laughed. "I don't know, but I'm only using weights tonight."

When he left the room, presumably to go change, I took my backpack and the shopping bag of notes over to the sofa and started unpacking. Neatly, however, so that he could easily move things aside and still feel like he had a living space. I flipped open my laptop and searched for his network. I had just finished opening up all the documents I needed when he walked back out of the bedroom in gym clothes.

"I'll be back in an hour," he said casually.

"Wait," I stopped him. "What's the password for your wifi?"

"Ah, the network is SGX54 and the password"—he looked vaguely embarrassed—"is HarridanSecrets."

I laughed.

I looked over my list from that afternoon, trying to decide my next steps. In the last year, I'd made important headway in my research, at least if I wanted to do a comprehensive biography of Anne Gracechurch's life, which was something that had never been done. Despite the one survey of English women's literature that had mentioned her seventeen books, apparently no museum or library had been interested in her life and work thus far except in the way she reflected on other, more famous authors and artists, at least none that I had discovered in the last twelve months of calling archivists and searching online catalogs and the internal-use-only catalogs that had been e-mailed to me. Luckily, a decent portion of her books had been digitized and archived online. Otherwise, maybe I never would have stumbled across her and the mystery of her connection to James Mead.

I'd found two other English dissertations that dealt with Gracechurch in some way, and one history dissertation, but they each touched on her in only the most superficial of ways. If I did go with plan B, I could possibly examine her work in cultural context. Over and over she appeared at the fringes of other literary figures' lives, a letter exchanged here, a reference to her being at a dinner or a party there. In that case, James Mead would likely stop being a part of the story.

While I'd identified the location of at least some of her letters and papers, and even paid for copies of as many as I could to be sent to me, I was still vainly hoping to find some that had not yet been delivered to museums or archives. But as the last two days had proven, I'd hit a bit of a dead end with her family. So it was time to turn yet again to her social circle, as it was possible that someone else's family might have passed down private correspondence rather than commit it to the care of an institution.

Of those descendants who were easily found, I'd contacted several over the last few months. There were also a half dozen people whose genealogy I still needed to track. I was a little dizzy with the effort of keeping it all in order in my head.

"Going well?"

I looked up at Sebastian, blinking, as if I'd just risen out of a tub of mud. I hadn't even heard him come back in.

"I'm just going to shower off, but . . ." I knew he was speaking, but the mere word *shower* had me thinking of him naked, of tasting him, holding him in my mouth.

He was silent. Waiting for some sort of response from me. I shook my head. "A shower would be good. No! I mean, yes, it's going well."

His lips curved into a bemused little smile and he left the room.

I looked back at my computer screen. Stared at the document open in front of me. Listened to the sounds of him moving about the apartment. Going into the bathroom. Turning the shower on. Naked by now, for sure. I blinked to refocus my eyes, to make the print on the screen turn into actual words in front of me. There would be time enough for sex later.

If I could only tell that to the growing heat between my legs.

I looked at the clock in the upper-right-hand corner of my computer screen. It was after ten already. What would Sebastian do when he got out of the shower? Sit down and read? Go to bed? Invite me to join him? I was in the middle of his living space. If he wanted to watch television, would he feel like he was disturbing me?

I heard the shower stop, him puttering around the bathroom, then the bathroom door opening and his footsteps into his bedroom. Then there was a sound that seemed a lot like him lying down on his bed. Hmm.

He'd mentioned earlier the clean sheets for the sofa bed. Maybe he really intended to sleep alone. To abstain from sex. Despite the fact that he'd half seduced me into staying with him last night.

I shut the laptop and stood up. We'd have to have this talk, awkward or not. It would be even more awkward if we let potential misunderstandings grow.

HE WAS LYING on his bed, over the covers, wearing nothing but low-slung pajama bottoms and reading a book. His hair was still damp from the shower, and he had a towel behind him protecting the two pillows he'd used to prop up his head.

He looked sexy and comfortable and . . .

"Hi," I said. He looked up, interest clear in his gaze.

"You . . . don't have to hide away in here if you want to use the living room for any reason." I felt so stupid, like I was saying the wrong thing.

"I promised you a quiet space to work," he said. He laid his book—something about artificial neural networks—flat on his chest. Which made me focus on that chest.

"Yes, but I also don't want to inconvenience you."

"You're not. In fact, by helping me out, you're giving me more time to work on other projects."

Other projects? Like other secret clubs or things that had to do with that rather dense-looking book resting atop his body? But that wasn't why I was standing in his room, very aware that he was watching me intently and that I was having trouble meeting his eyes.

"Also . . . about the sofa . . ."

"Oh." He put the book aside and started to stand up. "Do you need me to show you how to open it?"

"No!" He stood still. Stared at me. "No," I repeated more gently. "Are we really going to pretend?"

"Mina." His expression was of the utmost seriousness and I started to regret the conversation. Maybe there was a more subtle way to have gone about this. But I was like a freight train—"I don't want you to feel like you have to have sex with me because you're staying here."

My eyes widened. Like I *had* to have sex with him? Tell that to my libido. The part of me that had decided that since I'd already broken the seal, so to speak, on having sex with him, I might as well fully enjoy myself.

"Not that I don't want to," he said quickly. "But . . . I didn't think last night about how everything might change."

The politics of power. He wanted to make certain it was even, that I was making my own choices.

"I don't really want to sleep on the sofa," I said softly. "I want . . . what you promised me last night."

He nodded and then smiled that small, secretive, little smile of his. "Excellent."

The shift was instantaneous, a transformation from concerned, cautious, and respectful to sexually magnetic and demanding. Every inch of him radiated intensity as he stepped toward me. He lifted one hand to my cheek, stroked my skin. "This is it then, Mina. I won't be so polite again."

I shivered at his words, not from fear but from anticipation, and nodded. I'd consented to something unspoken, beyond what I even fully understood. But I wanted it. I wanted to know him at his most raw, his most animalistic. I wanted . . . everything.

Chapter Seven

As I was going to be there indefinitely, or rather, as long as partway through August, I filled his fridge with all my favorite healthy snacks as well as food to cook for dinner. After all, we could hardly eat takeout every night. Then I'd spent the rest of the morning reorganizing my notes and rereading the rough sketches of chapters that might or might not make it into the final draft of my dissertation. Often I started in outline form, which quickly evolved into writing whole paragraphs.

By early afternoon I had three new pages full of questions that needed answering, loose ends and holes that needed filling. Above all, I still needed proof. But I was slowly building my case, even if it was mostly circumstantial.

I had a chronology of Anne's life. Quotes from letters about her work. And there were snippets that referenced subjects touched only in the Mead books in the years directly before the first Mead book had been published. Not only that, but her life had changed. She'd lost a child. She and her husband had ended up on different ideological sides of social justice.

For the first time in a month, since I'd realized that my time in England was running out, I felt optimistic about succeeding. Thanks to Sebastian.

Maybe it rankled that I needed to accept his generosity and ambiguous employment, but it also was healing. This was the Sebastian I'd thought I knew.

Which made me feel guilty, and I turned my attention to the Harridan House project, as I'd coined it in my head.

I opened the document Sebastian had e-mailed me. Then laughed. Obsession was right. Sebastian was limited only by time, certainly not by creativity. He'd clearly spent the few hours he did have mining the Web for any snippet of info.

Apparently, he'd started with his family. There was a list of all living descendants of his grandfather and then a list of his grandfather's sister's living descendants, all of whom had denied knowledge of a club called Harridan House.

For a moment I lingered on the family tree. Sebastian was the youngest of three siblings, born a decade after the next youngest. His father and brother were no longer alive, but the reason wasn't written anywhere. Which made sense in terms of the document's purpose but certainly didn't help satisfy my curiosity: When had his father died? When had his brother died? How had that loss affected him?

His sister had two children, but neither of them had been questioned. Presumably because they were still minors, and if their mother had no knowledge of Harridan House, then why would they?

There were no birth dates listed anywhere. I did a quick Web search to place his uncle, the current viscount, at sixty-eight years of age. He'd claimed no knowledge of the club and, if the place had been destroyed and never rebuilt or reestablished, why would he have? Why would either of his children? Nonetheless, Sebastian had been thorough and asked everyone. Everyone except his great-aunt, by whose name there was a question mark. Interesting.

I jotted her name down in my notebook: Rose Felch nee Bosworth. A loose end to tie up.

After the family, he'd listed the results he'd garnered from a basic Web search. Zero. Not on any discussion boards, or blogs, or searchable historical archives. He'd looked through London businesses from 1800 through 1945. He'd searched for a list of buildings destroyed in the Second World War. A Wikipedia page (which I quickly brought up as well), was limited in scope and considering that, according to the Museum of London's Web site, one hundred thousand homes were destroyed in London during the war, Sebastian had determined this avenue useless.

Additionally, Harridan House wasn't listed on any

public list of private gentleman's clubs or any list of brothels, including travelers' guides to London.

A general search for Madame Rouge, as well, had unearthed nothing but a short story in a modern erotica collection that was unlikely to have any actual connection to the historical Madame Rouge.

I kept reading page after page, an outline of Sebastian's very organized thoughts. He'd said he built algorithms, and from the little I understood of the work of quants in finance, it seemed as if I was gaining a window into the methodical, obsessive world of Sebastian's mind.

A mind now obsessed with me. Or rather, with having sex with me.

I couldn't stop the pleased little smile that curved up my lips. It stuck around even when I finally closed my computer and settled on the couch with the first of his grandfather's journals to read.

I made it through a year of Oxford, through the account of his sleeping his way across the college town, then the young girl he'd gotten pregnant (*why didn't Sebastian mention any of that fascinating gossip in his rundown about his grandfather?*), and the subsequent back-alley abortion that was discovered by his father, resulting in a huge fight and much adolescent raging upon the page. It hadn't been the seventeen-year-old soon-to-be-viscount's promiscuity that had brought down his father's ire, but his carelessness with the family's reputation.

Then the uncle stepped in, which led to the Honorable Colin Bosworth's induction as a member of Harridan House so that he could do the proverbial sowing of his wild oats in a discreet place where there would be no unfortunate consequences.

It was like a television teen drama, full of wealth and vices, and by the time I heard the key turn in the lock shortly before eight in the evening, I was completely hooked. The energy I'd gained from reading redirected to the stunningly sexy man walking into the flat. My pulse raced with anticipation, like I was a newlywed housewife or something, not just a grad student crashing on a couch.

I sat up, placing the book aside on the coffee table as Sebastian closed the door behind him and dropped his messenger bag on what appeared to be its customary place on the floor.

"I see you met my grandfather," he said wryly, sliding off his shoes and walking toward me. There was something about seeing him in just his trouser socks that made me feel like he was illicitly undressed. Ridiculously Jane Austenish of me considering I was wearing yoga shorts and a tank top, with no bra, and was decidedly more undressed than him.

Which he obviously noticed from the glint in his eyes. Already, I'd come to know that glint and recognize it for the sexual interest that it was.

"I can't believe you didn't mention the drama!"

He laughed, even as he knelt on the floor and pushed my knees apart. "Has he attended Harridan House yet?"

I sucked in my breath with anticipation and barely managed to shake my head. But his hands were on my bare thighs, his long fingers looking perfect there as they slid up over the skin.

"I bought food ... for dinner," I gasped.

His thumbs reached the outer seam of my shorts. What was with this guy and my hormones?

"That's lovely," he murmured, "but what I want from you right now is a bit"—his thumbs grazed over the junction of my legs—"different." He bent down, and I stared at the back of his blond head just a moment before I felt his mouth on my inner thigh, oh God, and his tongue. I fell back against the sofa pillows and gave in. "You"—lick—"should wear"—lick—"these shorts"—lick—"every day." Lick. "But as much as I"—lick—"like them"—his fingers hooked on to the waistband and tugged down—"I'd like them better off."

I raised my hips, and he slid the offending cloth down, my panties with them. Then, he knelt back between my open legs. Lowered his head again. His mouth settled just above my knee, teasing me, as he started his impossibly slow but relentless journey up again.

I had no shame. Sitting there, bare-assed, on his couch, with him fully dressed in his suit, and his head nestled between my legs and his mouth—oh God, his mouth—

"You mentioned something about dinner?"

I turned my head languidly on the pillow to look at him. Sometime in the last hour we'd moved to his bed. I felt sated, boneless, and nearly brainless too. I could so easily drift off to sleep.

But Sebastian seemed energized. Sometimes an orgasm worked that way.

"Just some salmon, lettuce . . ." I waved a limp hand like that gesture could list all the ingredients I'd purchased that morning with my well-used credit card.

"That sounds delicious." As if he realized I had no intention of moving, he bent back over me and kissed me. Slowly, tantalizingly, until desire started humming through my body again. Then he broke away. "Up you go."

I shook my head and pushed myself off the bed. Making dinner was the last thing I wanted to do, and yet . . . when I'd purchased the food that morning, I'd wanted to cook for him, in some weird, latently domestic, feminine way.

I looked around briefly. Then I remembered that all of my clothes were in the living room.

I gathered them, cleaned up, then went to the kitchen. It was small but immaculate, the counter space uncluttered by anything other than a coffee machine and an electric kettle. I rooted around in his cupboards for all the things I needed and then set up shop.

I was acutely aware of where Sebastian was at all times, the bathroom, back to the bedroom, then doing something in the living room.

Then, leaning against the wall in the kitchen watching me. Like having a woman cooking for him was the night's entertainment.

"So, your grandfather," I said as I slid the salmon fillets onto the pan. The smell of the hot oil and seasonings alone were making my stomach growl. "Does he ever go to Harridan House with friends?" I was already thinking of his grandfather as a character in a book, which meant eternal present tense.

I turned to look at Sebastian, who was staring up to his left, at space, but doing that eyes-glazed-over-thinking thing. "Yes, I'm fairly certain. I didn't note those?"

I shrugged. "You might have. I'll check after dinner. Maybe one of those friends is still alive."

"Possibly."

There was a slight sound of reticence in his voice. I remembered his reluctance to hire an outside researcher.

"You can't be worried about your family's reputation with them. After all, these men would be as complicit as your grandfather."

"I wouldn't wish to embarrass anyone who might have purposefully put that life behind him."

"Or maybe they didn't. Maybe they stayed when your grandfather left. Maybe they know a bit more about what happened during and after the war. Why did Harridan House simply disappear? Or did it?"

As I flipped the salmon over, for the first time I considered the possibility of Harridan House simply having been moved. Perhaps it even still existed. Though how in today's modern age of social media a club could remain so secret that no one knew of it would be beyond me. And made its continued existence less likely.

I turned back to Sebastian with a sudden thought. "That's what you hope, isn't it?" He raised an eyebrow in question, but I knew he understood what I meant. "That's half your obsession. You *want* it to still exist." A flicker crossed his face and I knew I was right. "What would you do then? Fuck your way through it the way your grandfather did? The way the last two centuries of ancestors did?"

"It would be tempting." He took a step toward me. I held up the spatula like a shield.

"Uh-uh," I said quickly. "You don't get to deflect the conversation away by having sex with me."

He grinned, a guilty-as-charged grin, and there was another little insight into Sebastian. He used sex as a sleight of hand as much as an obsession. Interesting.

He still stepped forward, took my wrists in his hands. "I admit, I'd hoped." Somehow he had my hands, spatula and all, behind my back and his body pressed close to mine. It didn't matter that we'd emerged from his bedroom barely half an hour before. My breath quickened. The mound between my legs grew heavy with need. "But now, with you here . . ."

"You're an absolute slut," I whispered.

His answer was to press his lips to mine, to tease mine open, to drug me with his taste. Through his boxer shorts, I could feel him hard against me.

"And you like me that way."

I did, for now, as long as it didn't hurt me, didn't affect me in any way.

The scent of burning garlic made me twist away from him and pull the pan off the stove even as I turned off the burner.

"I think we should check into his friends," I repeated, trying to calm my overactive libido. "I also wonder if your family has any household records or correspondence that might be useful. Do they keep archives?"

"There might be. Likely, actually. I'll look into it."

Satisfaction slid through me as I finished making dinner. One day and I'd been helpful already.

Chapter Eight

I WAS STARTING to disbelieve that Sebastian had actually gone the last year and a half with only infrequent sexual encounters, or that he'd spent nearly the last six months entirely abstinent. I'd never known anyone so insatiable, and on Friday morning, with every muscle of my body aching, I was sore inside and out. Yet, I still wanted more.

But that was all I really knew about Sebastian. After reading through two of his grandfather's journals (which at one point had devolved into an almost pornographic description of some of his experiences at Harridan House), I was beginning to know more about the inner workings of *that* man's mind than about the man with whom I was sleeping. Sebastian avoided discussions about work, about the regular poker game that he said would keep him late on Fridays, about family (other than what was necessary for the research), and about any of his *obsessions* other than sex and Harridan House.

Why?

Not that it really mattered. I only needed to know what was relevant to the job for which he was paying me. The fact that we were having sex was a side matter, a perk and an indulgence.

Halfway through the morning, I put down his grandfather's journals and turned my attention to the mystery of Anne Gracechurch and James Mead. Which lasted all of ten minutes before I went to visit my usual Internet haunts and to check my e-mail.

There was yet another message from Sophie, who I still hadn't managed to connect with via phone, asking if I was okay.

I pressed reply, again. I'd done this a dozen times over the last few days but always ended up closing the e-mail without writing a word. Everything had changed since Sunday.

Everything.

But Sophie was the type who grew more convinced something horrible had happened the longer there was no communication. If I didn't want her asking the British police to hunt me down, I had to say something.

> Soph,
>   Staying longer. New situation . . . Will tell you everything when we chat. I'll be online most of the day.
>   M

I sent my mom a brief e-mail as well.

Bumped into a friend in England. Staying a bit longer. Research going well.

The question was, *which* research was going well? Gracechurch? Harridan House? Or my exploration of Sebastian's body and all the ways to give and receive pleasure?

A HOT TONGUE on my sex, licking, sucking, thrusting up into me— I woke in a shuddering, bucking orgasm, struggling against the hands that restrained my hips.

"Good. You're awake."

Cool air touched me where his mouth had been. I cracked my eyes open, still reeling.

"We have a drive ahead of us."

I closed my eyes again. Or maybe I'd never opened them. Maybe I was still dreaming.

Except the feel of his fingers pinching my oversensitized clit was all too sharp and real. I yelped and swatted his hand away. He had an unnerving tendency to treat my body like his personal playground. Not that I really minded, but—

His hands grasped my thighs firmly, pushing them back apart, and I knew, even before the heat of his body settled between mine, what was to come. With a contented sigh, I gave in to the hot length of him sliding into me. I could wake up this way every day. If only it weren't so early.

I reached for him, wrapping my legs around his hips and pulling his chest close to mine.

"What time is it anyway?"

"Six. We need to get to Yorkshire by luncheon, or my aunt will be very put out."

Yet he was still sliding in and out of my body leisurely, as if we had all the time in the world.

"Why didn't you tell me yesterday that we were going?"

"Because," he said, in as exasperated-sounding a voice as I had, "I didn't know we'd be going until this morning."

Which then, of course, led me to wonder how long he'd been up.

"No more questions," he muttered, moving a bit more roughly, and the force of the motion took my breath away. Which he'd clearly wanted. Then he pulled out abruptly and turned me over, running his hands over the curve of my backside even as he slid back in. As every thrust pushed me forward into the pillows, I realized the significance of this trip: first, I'd be meeting his family, second, I'd be visiting the estate of a viscount, and third, he must have learned that his family did in fact keep records dating back centuries, or we'd have no reason for the drive. Sebastian's fingers moved to the slick flesh between my legs, manipulating the small rise of flesh once more, and this time the release was harder, overwhelmed by his movements as he sought his own rising pleasure and by the weight of his body as he collapsed over me, pressing me down into the mattress.

THE FIRST HOUR on the road passed by in a blur of music and music podcasts, from Top 40 to drum n' bass. I fell asleep within ten minutes of being in the car and woke up on the M1 to Yorkshire with a stiff neck and surrounded by the incredible green of the countryside.

It felt good to be outside of London and on the road.

"Did you grow up there?"

"At Stanton Hall?" There was a bit of incredulity in his voice, as if the answer should have been obvious. "No. Mum did, of course, and we spent quite a few summers and breaks there, but she moved to London when she married."

"So your mother lives in London?" That surprised me a bit. I'd only been staying with him for a few days, and sleeping with him for hardly longer than that, but somehow the idea that he had family so close at hand didn't seem to fit. "Do you see her often?"

"No. She lives with my sister. In Manchester." He didn't elaborate when I waited for more. I wasn't particularly close with my own family. I loved them. They'd raised me well enough and done the best for me that they could on the salary of a Minnesota public-school teacher and a social worker, but in the last five years I'd visited my hometown once.

I wanted to know more. About his life, about what had shaped him to become who he was, but I wasn't certain how to delve deeper.

"Your sister's older, right?"

He glanced at me out of the corner of his eye. "She was the middle child, if that's what you wanted to know.

The way he said that made me feel horribly guilty, but I did want to know more. Like how his father and brother had died and how that had affected him.

Of course, I wasn't willing to talk about my life in great detail either. Then again, aside from the last two years that I had reason to want to obscure from Sebastian, my life was fairly ordinary. Both parents still living, middle-class, working hard in a world where the American Dream was proving over and over again to be a figment of the early twentieth century's collective imagination. My younger sister had stayed locally, pursuing a stable career as an accountant. She'd just gotten engaged, so likely a wedding would be a reason to return home soon.

We stopped off for a coffee and bathroom break at Newport Pagnell and then again, nearly two hours later, at Woodall. I wanted to get off the main road and explore, but we were on a schedule, and Sebastian assured me I'd have my fill of winding country roads when we exited the motorway north of Leeds.

The farther north we went, the thicker the cloud coverage and the more insistent the threatening shade of grey, until finally we were driving in a shower of rain, which I loved.

Just after 11 A.M., we reached our exit and headed toward Stanton Hall, near Wakefield in West Yorkshire, which meant little to me since I knew next to nothing about English geography. All I knew about Yorkshire, in general, was the literary people associated with it, from the Brontës to Ted Hughes to Tolkien. I had very romantic notions of the area, and so far, as we drove in this moody downpour, it was fulfilling my expectations.

It took us another thirty minutes of smaller and smaller roads before we pulled onto a long drive flanked with tall trees.

Excitement rose within me. I'd been to a few historical houses over the last few months, but this felt different. Here I'd have access not usually given to the public.

Here, I wasn't the public.

Stanton Hall was a fairly modest manor. As we came closer, Sebastian pointed out details about the house. It had been updated in the midtwentieth century to include all the modern conveniences, and then again in the last ten years. It currently boasted solar panels and a whole host of other environmentally friendly improvements. Despite the updating, its seventeenth-century bones were still apparent.

And there was *staff*. Like it was a hotel or something. From the moment we parked, there was someone to take our bags and hand us umbrellas. Perhaps I had once fantasized about living in a house like this, back when I was sixteen and reading *Evelina* or *Pride and Prejudice* for the first time, but I could no longer imagine it. Of course, no one could keep a house of this size clean or in good repair without the appropriate help.

Edie Bosworth, or rather, Lady Stanton, greeted us at the front door. Sebastian's aunt was a slim, petite, stylish woman of about sixty, in a silk wrap dress with dark hair cut into a bob, which showed off a pair of oversized diamond studs.

Or what *I* thought was oversized. Likely, they were all the rage amongst her set.

"Sebastian! Such a pleasure to have you here."

He bent down to accept her embrace and kiss on the cheek before stepping back to introduce me.

"It's lovely to meet you, Mina. Well, the two of you will have to tell me all about this mysterious research project over lunch. But before that, Sebastian, darling, you can have your usual room. I've put your guest in the pink room next door. Harry won't be back until dinner, so it's just the three of us."

I followed Sebastian up the staircase. A large painting of what looked like a young Edie, someone I assumed was her husband, and a dark-haired little boy, hung on the wall, and next to it were other smaller oil paintings. Of landscapes and of people I gathered were Bosworth ancestors. It all looked very traditional, and I wondered where they would hang the more modern art, assuming they had any interest in art outside of family heritage.

FOR LUNCH, WE sat down at the end of a dining table that could seat fourteen comfortably and possibly squeeze another two in if necessary. But the formality of the meal stopped at the decor. The cook, or maybe one of the maids, had set out an assortment of sandwiches and cold salads.

After a few brief questions about me and my visit to England, Edie switched to a discussion of family. Her sister had recently moved to Spain with her husband, a retired surgeon. Their children were all married with small children of their own, and I listened to a brief recital of how Marissa was studying Mandarin Chinese and Alex was preparing for his 11+ Common Entrance Exam.

"If you'd come up last weekend, you would have caught Lydia." This was Edie's youngest daughter. "But she's off again, to Bali."

"I saw her in London not too long ago," Sebastian said. "I went to her exhibit in March. We all had dinner."

"Nigel, too? He's in Monaco," she said.

"Naturally. The race is this weekend."

"I wish he'd settle down already. At this rate, I'll be seventy at his wedding."

"That's assuming he ever marries. I'm sure Ned will be more than happy to take on the burden of continuing the family name."

Edward Bosworth, I thought instantly. Sebastian's other uncle, who had three sons, both under the age of ten.

"Hmmph." Edie shot Sebastian a rather dirty look, and I wondered if their relationship was usually this tense and borderline acrimonious. It seemed odd, considering Sebastian felt right at home at Stanton Hall.

"So, what exactly are you researching, Sebastian?" his aunt asked, switching the subject.

"That private club Grandfather mentioned belonging to during the war. I was curious about it."

"Your grandfather." She shook her head, her lips twisting. "I don't now why he left all those ridiculous journals to you. He must have thought his life was fascinating, but he never left the estate. Not in the fifty years that I've lived here."

But Edie knew nothing about the young Colin Bosworth, who, according to his journals, had lived a quite scintillating life. I was curious to keep reading them, to see how he had charted his change from man-about-town to staid country gentleman.

We all had the capacity for change.

"And really, they should be in the library for posterity," Edie continued.

"The library you've been wanting to overhaul and throw into storage for decades?" Sebastian asked, clearly amused.

"As it should be," his aunt said defiantly. "Nobody uses the library or a single thing in it. This place is a mausoleum to the past, and it isn't even because we're limited by the National Trust. If we can have solar panels, why can we not have a modern interior?"

The topic seemed one that had been well trod, but it offered the beginning of an insight into Edie Bosworth, who, unlike my first impression, apparently felt stifled by the trappings of history, the burden of a title and an estate.

Sebastian shrugged.

I picked at my food, spearing individual peas on my fork and lifting them one at a time to my lips. This conversation wasn't my battle, and the only thing I needed to do was be polite, noncommittal, and available for research.

"In any event, whatever you want would be in the library or the attic," Edie said with a sigh, as if realizing her complaints had fallen on deaf ears, and there was no point in continuing.

Which meant it was time for me to start the polite part. "The drive from the M1 was so beautiful," I said brightly. "What are the cannot-be-missed sights in the neighborhood?"

AFTER LUNCH, SEBASTIAN walked me through the gallery, which was filled with more paintings of his ancestors.

"This is incredible." I tried to imagine Sebastian growing up here, spending his summers running about this huge house. My own childhood home could likely fit in the gallery alone. "Were you ever jealous? You know, that your family had to live elsewhere?"

"Yes and no." I looked at him in surprise. I hadn't really expected an answer. Sebastian usually avoided anything that delved beneath the surface. Beneath *his* surface; he'd been more than happy to listen to me fall apart earlier in the week. "I have a healthy respect for history. For my family's history, which no one else in the family seems to have."

Apparently, the estate had long since been whittled down to the bare bones to pay for debts incurred over the centuries. The current wealth came from Sebastian's late grandmother, who had been the heiress to a whisky fortune.

"Preservation is essential," he continued, "and England has its own unique approach to melding its history with the present day."

A history I was fascinated by, or I wouldn't have spent my time studying nineteenth-century English literature. Yet, the older I got, the more perspective I had, and maybe even the more I struggled financially, I found myself slightly resentful of the idea of an inherited monarchy in modern times that owned so much of a country's land.

As if he could read my thoughts, Sebastian continued. "At the same time . . . I think aristocracy as a measure of self-worth is ridiculous. Wealth begets wealth. It is much easier to stay wealthy and privileged than it is to get there from nothing."

Nothing being where I came from. Nonetheless, I'd never wanted *wealth*. Sure, I'd daydreamed about castles and manors when I was a child, but I just needed enough—enough to not have to worry, to be comfortable. To finish my dissertation and achieve the very academic dream of graduating and finding a university position.

"Wealth also apparently begets depravity. At least in your family," I teased. "So let's get down to business.

We found the household estates in the library, where most of the bound family documents were kept. Big leather tomes. Loose items, such as correspondence, were potentially in the attic. Which was not particularly good news as heat rose, and the ravages of time were more likely to be visited upon items stored in a non-air-conditioned space at the top of the house.

"I very much doubt the annual membership was paid out to 'Harridan House,'" I said dryly, one of the books heavy in my lap. "From all the research you've done so far, I'd guess whoever collected the funds wanted it to seem as innocuous as possible, so we're looking for holding companies, trusts, names of solicitors."

"Which could be hundreds, if not thousands, of entries for each year."

"Yep. But if we compare that long list from the year your grandfather last frequented the club to the year after, we should find where they no longer overlap. Which should be a much smaller list."

I handed him the volume for 1942 and 1943, being the one resting on my thighs. Then I retrieved a notebook and pen from my backpack and gave it to him.

"And this would be why I've enlisted your services," he said, taking the items obediently.

I pulled my laptop out and opened it, starting a new document for my list.

I slanted a glance over at him. "I think you just wouldn't get the same perks and the all-inclusive service if you used a professional researcher."

"Oh, I don't know about that. I'm fairly persuasive."

"Ew."

He laughed. "Contrary to what you believe, I don't sleep around with every attractive woman I meet."

I looked at him doubtfully. "I really don't know how you remained celibate this year. I've never known anyone with a sex drive like yours."

Of course, as far as these next months went, I liked his

sex drive. I enjoyed waking up to his mouth between my legs and the way he was ready for rounds two and three the same night. Just thinking about it turned me on, but I ignored the growing heaviness of lust and focused on the task at hand.

We sat in the library, each in a huge, wingback, hunter green chair, for what seemed like hours.

Luckily, the steward of the estate had been extremely detail-oriented. For the most part, it was easy to dismiss the great proportion of business and bills as normal household expenses. Payment for a membership to another gentleman's club buoyed my spirits that most likely Harridan House was encoded somewhere in here. Or rather, in Sebastian's volume.

At five, a woman dressed in a black-and-white maid's uniform popped her head in and asked if we'd like to join Lady Stanton for tea. Sebastian gave our apologies, and instead, the woman, Sara, returned with a heavy tray of tea, scones, and cookies, or rather, biscuits. Except thinking of the cookies as biscuits made me want real biscuits, fluffy buttermilk starch swathed in butter and jam. I moved the books off my lap and settled for a scone with clotted cream and raspberry jam.

"This, I could live with," I said after the first heavenly bite. "As long as I also had access to your gym."

Sebastian laughed. "The cook is one thing I am jealous about, actually. Trevor's been with the family for at least as long as I've been alive. I always had a growth spurt after summer."

I snacked over the next two hours, unable to stop

myself from reaching for the tray again and again, even as I made progress through the accounts. By dinnertime, I wasn't hungry at all, but when we sat down with Sebastian's aunt and uncle at that same long dining table, the John Dory cooked in butter enticed me anyway. It was as if, after four months of barely subsisting on the cheapest food available, I'd been presented with a feast.

Like Sebastian, his uncle was tall, a trait I assumed ran in the family. Unlike his wife, he didn't spend more than a minute inquiring about our afternoon activities, and despite his alleged lack of interest in the history of the estate, he certainly sounded invested in its future. He was passionate about green initiatives and active in promoting local developments in energy efficiency and sustainability.

"Worth investing in," he said pointedly to Sebastian.

"I don't work at the energy trading desk," Sebastian replied noncommittally.

Of course, that segued into a conversation about investments and what Sebastian did actually do, which generally had to do with creating proprietary models for determining prices and managing risk.

It was funny to think of his uncle, who downed glass after glass of wine with his meal until his face was almost alarmingly pink, as a viscount. Until that day, the aristocracy, people who held titles, seemed so much more the stuff of history and literature. Yet, here I was sitting at a table with Lord and Lady Stanton, the whole situation somewhat surreal.

When the meal was over, Sebastian suggested a walk.

His uncle waved us on as if he was much happier to not actually have to entertain anyone for a moment more.

It was chilly outside, much cooler than London. Despite my sweater, I shivered as I followed Sebastian outside into a night sky that was the royal blue of just past sunset. We strolled along a path on which solar garden lights illuminated our way.

To a wall of hedge that was draped with twinkle lights.

"They have a maze." It was like a cliché of what an Anglophile such as myself would have wanted in a dream home.

"Indeed," Sebastian said with a hint of humor. He took my hand, and there was something so tender in the way he held me that I clung to him as I followed. "Most of the acreage has long since been sold off, but the gardens and some of the woodland remain. I'll show you tomorrow before we leave."

Despite the near dark, he seemed to know his way, making each turn decisively. With his warm hand holding mine and the twinkle lights and scent of evergreen fragrant in the air, it was an utterly romantic moment. One that could lull me into believing I was there under different circumstances, in a relationship or maybe even in love, and that the future held promise.

The hedges opened into a wider space that enclosed a fountain and a bench. We sat, and I shivered again when the cold stone cut through my jeans. Sebastian noticed and pulled me close to him. I glanced up and melted under the look in his eyes. Almost—

I looked away.

"Your aunt and uncle seem nice," I said, staring at the fountain, a very neoclassical sculpture of a woman draped in diaphanous clothes. I tried to find identifying features that would reveal if she were a nymph or a goddess or some other mythological entity, but time had worn away at the cheeks, hands, and feet.

He laughed. "*Nice* isn't exactly the word I'd use for them. *Entitled*, perhaps. *Self-absorbed*."

"Damning words."

"Truthful words."

"And you're not?" I challenged. Although, as much as *entitled* seemed somewhat accurate for Sebastian, *self-absorbed* did not.

"I am," he admitted with a shrug.

"So are you 'not nice' either?" I pushed further, not certain why I was needling him, but sitting here, in the fresh air, under the ridiculously romantic night sky, I wanted more from him. I wanted what he hinted at when he'd clasped my hand within his or when he looked at me as he had only a moment ago. Maybe I even wanted the charming, self-effacing grad student I'd crushed on. "I still remember when you told me how fast you wanted to make your millions."

He laughed. "But at least I want to *make* the millions and not inherit them."

I didn't know exactly how much he made now, but I did know that he worked long hours, and in the evenings he often spent his "free" time working on algorithms and reading about neurology, psychology, and artificial intelligence, casting a wide, interdisciplinary net for his pet projects. His obsessions. He was driven. There was something admirable about that pursuit.

And yet . . .

"In finance . . . aren't positions like yours, companies like the one you work for, a big reason for the lingering recession and financial instability in Europe and the US? Banks getting bailed out again and again simply because they are 'too big to fail' and then ruining things for the rest of us?" I was pushing him, at the edge of my limited understanding of the early-twenty-first-century financial crisis, of the impact of quantitative analysis on Wall Street and on the rest of us. Hardworking people like my father, whose retirement funds had suffered a drastic setback through no fault of his own.

"I'm not going to argue the morality of it all, whether our actions cause instability or stability in the market," Sebastian said softly. "But I enjoy the mystery and the challenge. I like finding solutions to mathematical questions, developing new ways to model behavior. However, one of the biggest problems is that people make the same mistake over and over again. They forget to take into account freak situations, extreme moves. They forget the power of human fear. But when we learn from the past . . ."

He didn't need to finish. I knew the old adage: *Those who do not study the past are condemned to repeat it.*

"And people aren't making those same mistakes now?"

"I'm not," Sebastian said decisively. But he said nothing about the others. The great swath of investment bankers and hedge-fund managers. Of all the people like him who played with risk, all in the pursuit of money.

I shivered. He pulled me into his lap, wrapped me up in his arms, where I rested my head against his chest and listened to the constant trickle of water from the fountain. To the muted beating of his heart.

"No," he said after a long while. "I'm not nice either."

I DIDN'T SPEND the night in the pink guest room. Instead, I spent it wrapped in Sebastian's arms in the big four-poster bed in which he'd spent so many summers since childhood. But naked and entwined, we weren't children.

I woke up before he did and lay still, listening to his deep, even breathing and the sounds of a strange house rousing on a Sunday morning. I had no idea what time it was, but I was eager to get to work, to peek into the attic and take a first survey of all the family correspondence. Since Seb had work in the morning, and we had to drive the several hours back to London, we only had a few hours to make progress.

"Wake up," I whispered, lifting my hand to stroke his cheek, feeling the roughness of the stubble there. I leaned forward and pressed a kiss where my hand had been.

He shifted, his eyelashes fluttering slightly.

"Time to wake up," I repeated, trailing my fingers down his neck. His hand caught mine, stilling its progress, and his eyes were open, or somewhat cracked open, as he squinted at me. Then he pulled my hand lower, under the covers, his lips curved in a smile. I shook my head at him as my fingers wrapped around his morning hard-on. "Uh-uh," I said, even as I stroked him. "We don't have time for this." I released him and rolled away, slipping from the bed before he could grab me.

He made some sort of grunt, then I heard the flop of his arms as they fell back against the pillows above his head. I ignored him, gathered my shirt and jeans from the night before, and crossed through the restroom that connected my room to his. My backpack was in the pink room, and I'd need to go there to change into fresh clothing.

I was washing my face when he joined me in the restroom, dressed but sleepy-eyed. He stood behind me and pressed his hips against mine. He was still hard and desire flooded through me. He cupped my breasts through my shirt. To steady myself, I lowered my hands and rested them on the countertop, even as water dripped from my face down into the sink. But when the water trickled down my neck and chest, making my shirt damp, I reached for the towel, slapping his hands away.

He released me with a sigh and reached for his toothbrush.

I was happy with the progress we'd made the day before. When we arrived back in London, I would take the lists of unaccounted-for vendors and expenses and compare them with each other in the hopes that I'd find Harridan House listed under some alias. While there was more we most likely could look through in the library, now that I knew what sort of information was available there, I wanted to start cataloging the papers in the attic before we headed back to London. That way I'd know if it made sense either to take anything back with us or to return the following weekend for more. If the ledger strategy I'd suggested didn't work, then it would make sense to look through the older records.

The attic was stunning and far more cluttered, though in a fairly orderly way, than the addition behind the Mallards' house. One glance revealed layers of history and, luckily, the most recently stored materials were obvious and labeled in plastic storage bins.

I wrote down the names of all the people with whom he'd corresponded, to check it against the list of friends who had accompanied Colin Bosworth to Harridan House, but none of the letters referenced the club at all. In fact, if we hadn't read the journals, it was unlikely we'd ever have imagined that he'd spent a few years of his life dedicated to complete hedonism.

Until, at about ten in the morning, when the sun was finally starting to shine through the windows and heat up the room, we found the faded black silk half mask with the small gold-embroidered letters HH. Out of context, the item would have meant nothing, perhaps been thought part of a costume for a masquerade, but there it was in front of us: tangible proof that this club had existed outside the pages of one man's journal.

Sebastian fingered the silk carefully, his eyes alight with excitement.

Then he reached for me, caught me at the nape of my neck, fingers intertwining with my hair, and kissed me. I understood this kiss, one of excitement over our discovery, and yet, I so wanted it to mean more.

But for Sebastian, this was the ultimate treasure hunt. He spent his days searching for truth in numbers, for the essence of finance. He loved the hunt, the search, the relentless progress toward a final goal, even with all the circuitous twists and turns that cropped up along the way. And I did too. As frustrated as I was with being stymied in my Gracechurch research, I enjoyed the moments of discoveries, the feeling of being on the trail of something great.

This little scrap of cloth was our gold.

We worked with renewed vigor after that. Despite that find, we were still far from any sort of concrete progress. Yet Sebastian didn't seem bothered by that. Had he had an equal lack of urgency about his research before I'd agreed to help? Or was it that now that he'd delegated this "obsession" to me, he was free to pursue others, lessening the intensity?

We stopped at lunchtime, after which we had to head back to London. I was surprised when, instead of sitting down to eat with his aunt and uncle, Sebastian picked up a picnic basket from the kitchen and led me outside.

"I want to show this to you before we go," he explained as we trekked across the lawn, over a stile and stream, and through a small copse of trees. I was amazed at how large the estate still was despite the years of selling off land.

Finally, we came to a meadow with the stone ruins of a castle.

"It's not real, of course," Sebastian said. "Or rather, wouldn't have been real when it was first built two hundred years ago. Faux ruins of a Norman castle. Now it has its own history."

I loved it. We were still high on our find of that morning. Somehow the day was more beautiful, the grass greener, and this folly that much more magical. I helped him lay out a large woolen plaid blanket over a flat patch of grass and started to open the basket.

"We used to play here every summer. My sister, Lydia, and me. Nigel, sometimes, when he felt like humoring us. Sometimes Ruby and James, or Matthew." The last were all second cousins from Rose Felch's line. "Hide-and-seek, it."

"It . . . like tag?"

"That's right," Sebastian said, a familiar glint in his eye, and my whole body tensed in readiness for flight. He reached for me, but I was off already, stumbling over the grass and fallen (or carefully placed) stones. Of course, I'd only made it as far as the outer wall before he grabbed me by the waist. I squealed as he pulled me back, struggling, my gasps warring with laughter.

"Stop. I've caught you. You're mine."

His. With his other hand he fumbled with the fastenings of my jeans, then thrust his hand down the front, under my panties, grabbing me, fingers sliding between my lips and up. His touch was rough and shocking. I struggled again, this time to turn around so that I could be an active participant in this new game. But his fingers slid up and inside me, two of them pushing in and out, the motion limited by the constricting fabric of the jeans.

"I'm sure your games weren't nearly this X-rated as a child."

He laughed. "Oh no. Games are much more fun as an adult." He withdrew his fingers, leaving a damp trail along my belly as he dragged them up. Then he lifted his hand, past my cheek. We were so close that I could smell myself on him, just before he sucked his index finger into his mouth and slowly drew it out. "I love the way you taste. Like sex, primordial."

He slid his hands back down, over my breasts, my waist, hips, and then he turned me around. Took my hand in his and led me back across the clearing and into the folly's inner circle of stones.

"I've always wanted to do this." Sex here, I assumed, until I saw the big stone worn away by time so that its top was near flat. Centered in the middle like some sort of sacrificial table.

"*Someone* had kinky games they wanted to play here," I noted.

"One of my brilliant ancestors, naturally." He positioned me in front of the stone. "I've always wondered about the ancestor who had this created. Why he chose to move this rock here and if it was ever actually used in any ritualistic way." Whether it had or hadn't been, it was certainly about to be used creatively. "For a virgin sacrifice, you're wearing far too many clothes."

"It's chilly," I said, amused. "And I'm not a virgin."

"We can pretend." He tugged my jeans down my legs, stymied for a moment by my sneakers, but then pulled those, the jeans, and my panties off. I shivered

"Would you have liked that? To be my first?"

"Perhaps. I think I would love to have seen your face the first time you were penetrated. The first time you reached orgasm. Arms up."

"My first time hurt, and there was blood everywhere," I said flatly, my voice somewhat muffled through the wool of my sweater as he pulled it over my head.

"Then we'll have to make up for that this time. Although the blood might have been useful to appease whatever deity we're sacrificing you to."

Standing there naked, I was acutely aware that despite the noon hour, the sun hadn't warmed away the chill of the night or the previous day's rain.

"Come here." He lifted me up to sit on the stone, which was also cool still from the night. I shivered.

"We'll get you warm soon enough." He stripped out of his own clothes. I noticed the condom he pulled out of his pocket and set on the stone before he tossed the pile on top of mine. Always prepared for sex.

"I doubt those were part of the ritual," I said, but my gaze was trained on his erection, on his beautiful, hard length. I was on the pill and, as we'd discussed, I'd been tested before I'd left for England, but it hadn't been more than six weeks after the last guy I'd fucked, so there was no way I could say for certain I was a hundred percent disease-free. For both of us, it was better to be safe than sorry. Even if I did have an overwhelming desire to know how he'd feel inside me completely bare.

"Lie back."

I did, and with more surface area now touching the

stone, I shivered even more. He moved to my side and stroked my neck with his hand. "Shh," he said, his voice low and soothing. "This is your duty."

My duty as the sacrifice.

My nipples were hard already from the cold, and when he closed his mouth over one, the heat was nearly painful in contrast.

He worked his way down my body, ensuring this duty was a pleasure, and soon my shivers weren't all from the cold. I writhed on the smooth stone, fingers moving down, needing to ease the growing pressure. But he pushed my hand away, pulled my hips to the edge gently. Then his mouth was there, tongue sliding up my folds, parting me and delving within. He feasted on me like he loved it, and maybe he did. After all, I loved his cock in my mouth—funny how it was always a cock to me when I thought of oral sex, everything harder and more forceful—I loved the taste of his semen and knowing that I could take everything from him.

His lips closed on my clitoris, and his tongue's probing was replaced by fingers. One, then two. My legs tensed. I was close, so close. Then, for a moment, there was only cool air on my damp flesh, before he was back, his hips perfectly aligned with mine.

"Look at me."

I opened my eyes and lifted my head a bit to look down the length of my body at where he stood poised to enter, the tip of his cock pressing against me. I met his gaze, dark and intense, focused entirely on my face. Our eyes locked, he pressed in, parting me, filling me.

I gasped when he suddenly thrust forward, sinking into me fully, deep. My head fell back, eyes closing even as I reached for him, wanting to wrap myself around him.

"Look at me," he repeated, demanding, and I forced myself to lift my head again as he slid out and then back in, pushing me into the stone. His hands gripped my hips, nearly lifting me when he wanted deeper access, and I aided his goal with my legs.

Then he shifted, moved one hand to my clit, moving more slowly as he played with the little rise of muscle and nerves, gaze still focused on mine. I came suddenly, almost unexpectedly, my upper body arching against the stone, eyes closing. I heard a growl a moment before he was slamming into me hard, fucking me even as I was still shaking with the remnants of orgasm.

"Fuck!" I heard the word distantly as he came, pushing my knees up against my chest, leaning over me.

His breath was ragged, but his mouth was hot and open on my breasts. I peered at him between half-mast lids, at his blond head bent over me.

We rested there for a moment more, until finally he pulled out, slipped off the condom, and picked me up in his arms.

"Maybe it was fated for us to run into each other at the archives, or maybe it was just lucky chance. Either way . . ." His voice drifted off as he laid me down on the picnic blanket and then, this time far more gently, made love to me all over again.

Hours later, as we drove down the tree-lined lane back toward the motorway, I knew that what Sebastian had said the night before was a lie. He was nice. Exceedingly so. It was just hard for me to reconcile everything I knew about him with the way I'd blamed him for my "dark ages" all this time. It meant that at some point I was going to have to sit down and take a hard look at myself and my actions.

And that wasn't something I really wanted to do.

Chapter Nine

THE DAYS BEGAN a delicious sameness, a domestic normalcy: Sebastian off at work until late, me following leads on both the Gracechurch and Harridan House projects, then a shared dinner whenever he came home followed by sex. Or sex followed by dinner. Or sex, followed by dinner, followed by more sex. Interspersed between satiating our appetites, we discussed the research, or the news, or any random thing. Or I worked more, and Sebastian sat at his laptop, plugging away at some other project. He seemed calmest when he was doing something, whether it was fiddling with numbers (not that he'd appreciate that description of his activities) or sex.

And then Sebastian's cousin showed up, back in town after the trip to Monaco, which had been followed by a detour in St. Tropez.

"My cousin," Sebastian said, looking up from the text on his phone, but there was a wealth of backstory behind his mild words. I could hear it in the restrained tone that I was coming to know so well.

"The Honorable Nigel Bosworth," I said, remembering from the notes on his family.

Sebastian smirked. "Right. *Honorable*, such an interesting word, so liberally used."

"What, he's not nice either?" I wondered what it was about his family that made Sebastian's judgment of them so severe.

"Oh, he's nice enough. But *honorable* is a far weightier word. I'm not certain the Bosworth family, or the Grahams for that matter, know its definition."

Interesting that his criticism extended to himself as well.

"And we're going to dinner with him?" I pressed.

"He wants to meet you. The American girl I've shacked up with." He added the last with a smirk.

Not quite the detailed description of their relationship that I'd hoped for. "Why?"

"Because you're staying here, and you're helping me research a sex club." Sebastian shrugged as if his cousin's interest should have been obvious, but somehow I was a bit stunned at how cavalierly he'd been discussing this with his cousin.

"You told him?"

I'd known that he'd at least mentioned Harridan House to much of his family but had assumed he hadn't gone into details if they didn't recognize the name.

"If anyone in my family would have known about the club, it would have been Nigel."

And that statement suggested to me that Nigel was cut from the same promiscuous Bosworth cloth as his grandfather and other ancestors. As Sebastian.

We took the car, which seemed an unnecessary expense and hassle considering our relative proximity and the ready availability of public transportation, or even of a cab if we were desperate. But we parked in a structure that was a block away from our destination.

Sebastian stopped me as I started to open the car door and instead reached over and rested his hand on my bare leg.

"I think you're a bit overdressed."

I'd put on the dress I'd worn to Ziva. If this continued, I was probably going to have to buy another outfit for going out, something that hadn't been a particularly big concern the first four months of my stay. Sebastian was almost casual, if one could call the elegant insouciance with which he wore no tie and the shirt under his fitted jacket slightly undone at the neck.

"You should have mentioned that when I still had the chance to change." I was confused and slightly irritated that he was even commenting on my clothes in any way other than positive.

But then he slid his hand under my dress, a little smirk curving his lips, and my irritation drifted away. When his fingers tugged on the elastic of my flimsy mesh thong, I lifted myself off the seat to assist him. I knew girls from school who'd gone around without underwear for all sorts of reasons. I'd seen the paparazzi shots of celebrities who, whether purposefully or not, bared their naked bottoms to the world as they slid out of limos en route to a club or premiere. But the only person who would know about this tonight was Sebastian.

And me.

I was wet just thinking about it.

WE MET AT a private club that catered to the entertainment industry, which apparently Nigel was enough a part of to be a member even though, from what Sebastian intimated, the most creative endeavor he did these days was choosing his newest model or actress girlfriend.

As we checked in at the front desk, I noticed instantly that everyone who walked by us had that certain "sheen," that level of polish that seemed to be innate in the famous. Not that I recognized most of the people around us, but I recognized that they *could* be famous, that their clothes, eyebrows, airbrushed features were all hallmarks of those the paparazzi chased regularly, who showed up on the covers of tabloids and all the Internet news sites that barely pretended to real journalism anymore. Maybe some of them weren't wearing underwear either.

We were sent up an elevator to the top floor of the building, where the club's restaurant and main bar were situated.

Nigel looked very similar to Sebastian. Some of the gene pool was quite dominant, from their height to the shape of the nose to the line of their jaw. But that's where the resemblance ended. In every other way, the older man took after his mother. Dark hair, blue eyes, fuller lips. It was obvious what had made him a successful model in his twenties and helped him continue to be a successful playboy in the years beyond. He was distinctly more classically handsome than Sebastian.

He also knew it.

"So, Mina," he said as we sat down. "How did you meet Seb?"

"Grad school."

"Were the two of you dating then?"

"We're not dating now," I said quickly. I didn't dare look at Sebastian. There was a time when a real relationship with him had absolutely been something I'd wanted. But things had progressed too slowly and then . . . well. What we had now was more of an intimate understanding. Like temporary fuck buddies. I took a deep drink of my raspberry lemon drop.

"But you're having sex."

I nearly spit the drink out.

"Yes, Nigel," Sebastian cut in. "We're having sex."

"And she's helping you research this club Grandfather belonged to?"

"That too."

"Well, if you find this holy grail of sex . . . assure me that I'll be the first to know." He scanned me with a rather lascivious look that had me shifting in my seat as if that could relieve the sudden heat that pooled between my legs with the movement. "Or we could always just head back to your place, coz. Knowing you and this whole situation, I've no doubt Mina is a right little goer. There's always another poker game next week."

"To which I wasn't invited? I'm insulted." I stared at the two of them, a little stunned that in the wake of Nigel's casual suggestion that we all have sex, all Sebastian cared about was a poker game.

Apparently depravity *did* run in the family.

Nigel slanted me that hot glance again. "What do you say, love? We send Sebastian off to play cards, and you show me exactly what you aren't covering with underwear right now."

My eyes widened and, indignant, I looked to Sebastian in alarm, but he didn't seem to notice anything amiss, that his cousin had just made a pass at me. That his cousin had correctly assumed I was completely bare beneath my dress. Was this sort of behavior what Sebastian considered nice but not honorable?

"Joking, love," Nigel said with a laugh, holding up a hand. "Well, not about the knickers." I winced inwardly, wondering with just how many women Sebastian had played this little game and what the purpose was. "I know my little cousin well. And I wouldn't let him near my friends with that wicked brain of his. He's even blackballed in Monaco."

I was sufficiently distracted by that little tidbit. "What, do you count at cards or something?"

Sebastian shrugged. He was definitely *not* the chatty cousin.

But later, after dinner, when we had stepped out to a small balcony overlooking the city, and Nigel had gone for drinks, Sebastian leaned close to my ear, his lips touching my skin. "Would you do it if I asked? Let me share you with Nigel?"

I stiffened. "Are you jok—"

"No?" He pulled me back against him, against his unmistakable arousal. "But you find him attractive. I want to know what your fantasies are, Mina."

"You're a perv," I whispered.

"No," he denied, licking my skin, making me shiver, "I just like sex. And I like sex with you."

I was wet and, bereft of my panties, which were stuffed in the glove compartment of Seb's car, I could feel the moisture on my upper thighs.

His hand was creeping up my dress, sliding over my bare skin. I held my breath in anticipation of his destination.

"Started the party without me, did you?" Nigel's amused voice cut through the haze of desire sharply. I pushed Sebastian's hand down and away before turning.

"You must be between girlfriends," Sebastian noted, reluctantly letting me turn but still pulling me close to his side. His body was warm against mine and I savored the feel of it.

"No, actually." For the first time that night I saw Nigel's expression turn serious. "In fact, I was going to talk to you about that later this week." His gaze flitted to me as if deciding whether or not he could talk in front of me. I didn't really see why not since he'd treated me much like an object most of the night. "I proposed to Kate in Monaco. She said yes."

Sebastian's hand fell away from me.

"Congratulations," I said with a cheerful smile, trying to imagine what kind of husband Nigel would be, if his lascivious talk was just that . . . talk, and he'd be faithful. His promiscuous grandfather had been faithful to the whisky heiress once he'd said his vows. Maybe that journey was a Bosworth trait as well.

"Kate Grinnell?" I knew the name. In fact, she was probably the one English actress I actually would recognize if put to the test. I'd been fascinated when I'd seen her on a late-night show displaying her prowess with American accents. She was an indie actress darling.

"Yes, coz, what other Kate would I be talking about?"

"Congratulations!" Whatever daze had fallen over Sebastian had apparently been broken, and he embraced his cousin. "Your mum will be thrilled."

"No doubt. Of course, she won't be as thrilled to learn Kate's three months along and we'll be having the wedding this August."

"Sometimes it takes the unexpected to move you in the right direction." There was a note to Sebastian's tone that made me study him sharply, trying to figure out the deeper layer of his words. Or maybe there was none and I was simply overanalyzing, English Lit-style.

"Sometimes," Nigel agreed, though he seemed to miss the subtext I still hadn't deciphered. "Listen, mate, I want you to be one of my groomsman."

An hour later we were walking back to the car, and I struggled to keep up with Sebastian's brisk pace.

"What's wrong?"

"What do you mean?" He'd put up a good show at the club, but the instant we were on the street, his mood had shifted.

"I mean, are you *not* happy for your cousin?"

Sebastian didn't slow and instead turned into the doorway of the parking structure.

"And what the fuck was it with all that talk, treating me like I'm some sort of escort, like I'm not even in the room."

Finally, Seb stopped, so abruptly I nearly collided with him. He pulled me close anyway, trapping me against the door. "That's who my cousin is. In fact, that's who I am. Some pervy bloke who suggests threesomes and *has* shared women with his cousin before."

But was that Sebastian? There was what he was saying, what he had proposed two years earlier, and then there was everything else I was learning about him.

His hand was on my thigh, pushing my dress up, and I looked over his shoulder in shock, hoping no one would stumble over us.

"And now he's not your wingman anymore?" I managed, even as his fingers found me, slid over my damp heat, parting me.

"I'm not *his*," Sebastian corrected. "He's my older cousin. More like a brother, really. You're so wet."

There was something else I wanted to ask him, but it was hard to think. I gasped as he thrust a finger up inside me.

"I would have fucked you on that balcony, but instead I'll fuck you here."

"I thought London had cameras everywhere. Isn't there some law against this?"

"Do you care?" With his fingers inside me, at that moment I didn't care much.

I shook my head, eyes closed, breath coming fast. Somehow, standing out in the cool night, knowing anyone could stumble upon us, made sensation that much sharper, made the rise that much faster.

Then he did something else with his fingers, hit the right spot in just the right way that had my knees buckling. "Just don't stop," I mumbled, and he didn't.

His mouth descended on mine, his tongue invading my mouth the way his fingers were, thrusting, searing. I came hard, hitting my head against the door as I clenched around his hand.

I breathed in deep and then let out a ragged breath when he slid his fingers out. He lifted his hand to his mouth, the scent of my pleasure heavy in the air as he licked his fingers. "Later, I'm going to lick your pussy," he whispered. "Just like this."

I moaned, and he steadied me, hands on my hips.

"I like Kate. But he's cheated on her before." Still reeling from the orgasm, it took me a second to make sense of the words.

"So you don't think he'll be faithful? Your grandfather was, even after all his Harridan House escapades."

"Yes, my grandfather was never unfaithful. Once he married, that was it. Even though he didn't love her." Apparently, this was something Sebastian cared about.

"So you don't approve?" Not that I did either, but somehow I'd imagined Sebastian to be a bit less judgmental, a bit more laissez faire where matters of the flesh were concerned.

"Kate deserves more. And now I'm supposed to stand up there and support the pretense."

There was a certain morality to Sebastian that grew clearer the longer I knew him, that made the attempt to understand him more complex. That made his critique of his family and his discussion of honor that much more intriguing. Was there some secret, or was it just the usual familial drama?

"I'm sorry about the dinner and about the way he talked about you." The apology startled me even more.

"So you wouldn't have wanted a threesome with him included, assuming no Kate?" I challenged.

"That's not really a fantasy of mine. Yes, I've done it." I nearly laughed. What *hadn't* he done? "There was this night in Ibiza . . ." He trailed off. "But those games, that's all in the past." I parted my lips, taking a breath to ask how far in the past. Had that night in New Jersey been part and parcel of some old Sebastian, or was he simply talking about escapades with Nigel? "I'd much rather watch you with another woman," he continued, and my lips closed shut. "But if that had been what you wanted . . ." He trailed off, his voice sounding tight, as if, despite his words, he wanted me to deny any interest in his cousin or having sex with him and another man. Interesting. Almost cliché.

"Not really a fantasy of *mine*," I quipped. And it was true. I could hardly deal with my past promiscuity. The last thing I needed was to experiment more.

He smiled, all signs of tension gone. "Yes, threesomes don't really seem to be your thing." His head dipped close to mine, his breath scented with a hint of the whisky he'd had after dinner. "But what *are* your fantasies, Mina?"

"Oh, I don't know. Being a virgin sacrifice, getting finger-fucked in the doorway of a parking structure."

He laughed and moved away, opened the door, and waited for me to pass through. "*Your* fantasies."

"If by fantasies, you mean the things I think about when I masturbate? Most of them I'd rather keep in the privacy of my own fucked-up imagination, thank you very much. There's a difference between what turns me on and what I really want to experience."

He shrugged. "That's true. Still. There's a whole world in between."

And without a doubt, that conversation was exactly why, an hour or so later, as I sought my release with Sebastian thrusting between my legs, I was imagining another man, who looked suspiciously like Sebastian's clone, filling my mouth. I came hard and fast . . . but that wasn't a fantasy I wanted to make reality.

On Monday, Sebastian was back in the office, and I hit the Internet again. I only left the apartment to get a latte down at the corner coffee shop, which was a luxury but one I could afford, considering I was practically a kept woman.

At six, he texted me that it would be a later night, so I made dinner, ate my half, and put his away for later.

Shortly after nine, when he finally arrived, I was back on the couch, this time working on the text of my dissertation, on the parts that would be similar regardless of whether I went with my original argument or the backup.

I looked up briefly when he walked in and offered him a smile. His tired smile in return made my chest flutter in an uncomfortable way, and I focused on the computer screen as he went about the apartment, dropping his computer bag, taking off shoes, disappearing into the bedroom to change.

Only when he sat down next to me and peered over my shoulder did I close the computer and give him my attention.

Funny little chest flutter again.

"How is it going?"

"Good, lots of progress. How was your day?"

"Some issues with the IT department, but otherwise the usual," he said simply.

By now I knew he wouldn't elaborate, so I thought through the Harridan House work I'd done. "I've finally finished looking up all the people Colin mentioned from the first year he attended Harridan," I informed him. The entire project had taken several days, including a return trip to the National Archives. "He could have blackmailed so many people. I mean, yes he didn't name people by their full names, but I'm sure to anyone in society back then, these descriptions would have given it away."

"We don't have the benefit of that same knowledge." Sebastian sounded disappointed.

"No, we don't. I did, however, make a list of all the other young aristocrats who were of his age and listed as having attended the same school, and I checked it against his correspondence. It's interesting your grandfather didn't enlist."

"Yes. His brother did, however."

And that brother had died.

I moved on quickly. "So I managed to narrow it down to a few possibilities, only one of whom is still alive, and he's not listed, or is, as you Brits say, ex-directory."

Sebastian laughed. "Naturally. Who is he? I'm sure we can find his contact info fairly easily."

"Marcus, Lord Young."

Sebastian eyes lit with recognition. "I know Garrett Simmons, who's in line for the title. I'll inquire." But as excited as he seemed, he also had that reticence.

"You know, if you feel uncomfortable disturbing a ninety-five-year-old man, I'm sure there are other clubs like Harridan House that exist today," I teased. "Certainly swinger's parties or even dungeons." I might have been innocent and naive two years ago, but I'd read my fair share of erotica.

He shot me an inscrutable look.

"You think that's what I want?"

I raised an eyebrow but didn't say a word.

He shook his head in disbelief. "That's what you think. That I want to go fuck a bunch of strangers."

It's what I'd done on my quest to be more like him.

"What? You're obsessed with sex, Sebastian."

"Right. The Bosworth legacy." His lips set into a hard line, and, with jerky motions that indicated pretty clearly he was not pleased with my observation, he stood, unfastened his belt, and slid it out from his pants. Oh God, he was undressing? Unfair.

"And you're not?" he demanded, opening his fly, pulling out his semihard dick.

Shock at the abruptness of his actions froze me for a moment, but I stared at him, licking my lips nervously. He was right. I was obsessed. At least with him. There was nothing more I wanted to do than be on my knees in front of him, tasting him as he grew bigger and harder.

In fact, he was growing under my gaze. I looked up to his face. He raised an eyebrow.

I slid off the couch and crawled over to him, not breaking eye contact. By the time I slid my lips over him, he was fully erect. The salty tang of precum met my tongue. I gave in with an internal sigh that seemed to release all tension, ease everything but the desire to taste him, feel him fully.

His hands tangled in my hair, and I relaxed more, wanting him to take over, to fuck me this way, the way I'd read it described in books or seen in a porn video, or even in his grandfather's memoirs. I wanted him hard and overwhelming.

Instead, he pulled away, knelt in front of me, and pressed his lips to mine.

"Don't judge me," he whispered. "And don't presume this is all about sex."

My mind swirled in haze of desire, trying to make sense of that. *Not all about sex?* Then what was that little battle of wills about? Why had he needed to prove that I was as depraved and obsessed as him?

"Okay," I said, breaking the kiss. "What then?"

"Getting to know each other."

I laughed. We knew everything we needed to know about each other for this little affair. In fact I'd told him too much that last night at my old flat, and he'd told me next to nothing about himself.

"I've never been to a dungeon," he offered, his hands slipping down to the hem of my shirt, lifting. Yet again, a topic about sex, disproving whatever point he was trying to make. "Have you? Are you a secret dominatrix?"

I rolled my eyes even as I raised my hands over my head to let him pull the tank off, my mind filled with an image of leather, whips, ridiculously high stiletto heels—the clichéd limit of what I knew about the BDSM lifestyle.

"I don't think so," he continued. "I think you're more of a submissive. I think you want to do everything I want." Like suck him off at the unbuckling of his pants and the simple raising of an eyebrow?

I shuddered, the feel of him still fresh on my lips, desire building. If that was the definition, then maybe.

He tugged down on the cups of my bra until my breasts were free to the air, to his gaze, to the warmth of his palms.

"It wouldn't have been this way between us two years ago." He tugged on my right nipple, which pebbled under his touch. But inside, I was freaking out at his continued monologue, at this new direction: the past. "Whether I'd asked you out properly, or if you'd said yes to my rather ill-advised suggestion. Either way. Take your shorts off."

I was a mess. Emotionally still responding to that mention of the past and then, suddenly, he gave an order, and my mind emptied of everything but that clear directive. Simple. Doable. I stood, slipped off my shorts and underwear, my bra as well. He stood, too, pushing his pants down and then off, unbuttoning his shirt.

I stood there, naked, trembling with desire and confusion, watching the slow reveal of his chest, of the defined but not overly developed muscles.

"Into the bedroom." I went, looking back over my shoulder, half-worried he wouldn't follow me. He seemed angry for some reason, but he was caressing himself as he walked, keeping himself erect. I was intensely jealous of his hand.

When I reached the bed, I stood there, directionless, and turned to him, waiting. We were role-playing maybe. Or perhaps there was some truth to what he had said. But either way, I needed him to tell me what to do.

"Knees," he said simply, and I fell instantly, led him into my waiting mouth with a distinct sense of relief, of coming home. His hands tangled in my hair again, but this time firmly, as if he didn't plan to let me go.

"Tanya was kinky," he said. I stiffened at her name, but he pushed more firmly, held me in place as his hips rocked back and forth. "She had these handcuffs she liked me to use. Actually, she had this whole toy chest. Dildos, vibrators."

I'd seen some of those toys when I'd accidentally walked in on her washing them in the bathtub. But why was he saying this to me now? He couldn't have been so oblivious that he didn't realize mentioning her would hurt me. Why was he being so cruel?

I laid my right hand over his and started to pull it away from my head.

"It was a game for her, but I think for you . . ."

I froze. Was he serious?

"I don't think it would be a game."

He was fucking my mouth and analyzing me. I was angry and turned on all at the same time. I dropped my hand from his and instead focused on his cock, on his balls, on stroking all his sensitive places and bringing him to the brink. On eliciting those delicious groans that made me know I had power, wasn't some weak person who had no control over her life.

When he stiffened, holding my head still, I gagged a bit at the force of him nearly against my throat and struggled to take the flood of his semen. After his grip loosened, and I'd swallowed, I stood and angrily pushed him away.

"You think talking about your other fucks is a turn-on for me?" I demanded. "You think I want to be tied up and used by you? We've both made it very clear that we like sex, but that's it, Seb. Don't mind-fuck me, too."

I turned away from him, ran my hand through my hair, and looked up helplessly at the ceiling. I'd put myself in an untenable position. I was living in his apartment. I couldn't storm away because I didn't have anywhere else to go, and changing my airline ticket yet again would involve more money I couldn't afford to spend.

"There's sex and then there's what's behind the sex, Mina." He laid his hands on my upper arms, pressed me close to him, wrapping his arms around me. "Two years ago, you wouldn't have jumped into bed with me on a first date. What changed?"

I swallowed hard. He'd been making a circuitous argument in response to my claim that he was obsessed with sex. All of this was his answer because he was too fucking perceptive.

"I had no idea you were so manipulative," I fumed. "You want some deep, emotional answer from me? Like I said before, Seb, studious Mina needed a break. And I've always been curious what if." It was half the truth. He wasn't getting it all. Not now. Maybe not ever.

"I want to know what's going on in your head," he whispered, and I tried futilely to understand that expression on his face. "I want to know every single thing about you."

Something about the words, his tone, strummed the despair in my chest. Once I would have loved him to say such a thing because it would have meant something far different. It would have meant he cared. But now there was this other element between us.

"Why?" I demanded. "I would think it's enough that I'm willing to satisfy every one of your desires. That you have a living, breathing sex slave living in your apartment." I reached for his cock, only semihard and still damp from my mouth, stroking it. "It's early yet, Seb. Tell me what you want me to do."

He pushed my hand away and stepped back, assessing me. He wanted to know what was in my head, but he was the mystery to me. Too much a mix of contrasts.

"You're not my sex slave," he said finally.

"But I was your virgin sacrifice, surely I can be a slave as well." I was still angry with him, but I was settling into the role, the eroticism of playacting. I was determined to turn him on, to make him use me again the way he seemed to think I wanted to be used.

He ran a hand through his hair and took a deep breath.

"It's not all about sex," he repeated. He turned away and I stared at his back.

What else then? There was nothing else between us.

I watched him pull boxers and a T-shirt out of his dresser. Pissed, I climbed onto the bed and lay down, hand between my legs. I knew exactly when he caught sight of me in the mirror. He paused and watched me for a moment. I closed my eyes and focused on the sensation of my fingers on my flesh, taking it slow. I moaned, even though I wasn't anywhere near that point yet, but this was partly for show.

The creak of wood beneath his feet and a slight breeze of air made me open my eyes again. The room was empty.

I could hear the distant clicking of the keyboard. He'd retreated to his algorithms. His tidy game of numbers.

I finished masturbating angrily, the climax unsatisfying, then rolled over to my side and struggled to understand why I wept.

Chapter Ten

I STAYED ANGRY with him for days, yet it didn't change how much I desired his body. He was pushing me, as if he wanted something more from me that I didn't understand, even as he gave nothing of himself. I watched him in the evenings, working on his computer on a series of seemingly endless calculations, while I worked on either the Harridan House research or on my dissertation, making sense of whatever information I'd gathered during the day. I focused on Anne Gracechurch's place at the nexus of several different social circles, her correspondence with renowned thinkers of the day, how they affected or didn't affect the subject matter of her stories. If only I could prove the James Mead connection beyond statistical doubt, then this whole thing would really leap to another level.

For four nights, I slept on the couch, making good use of the pull-out bed. Friday was poker night with his academic and financial friends who apparently weren't that welcome in casinos either, and the first evening that wasn't filled with tense silence as we both simmered with our own private emotions. But somehow having him gone was worse. He still wasn't back when I fell asleep after midnight, barely managing to turn off the television, which I'd used to drown out the complete solitude.

When I woke abruptly, it was dark in the apartment, the only light the intermittent green glow of the power cord on my computer. But there was something different about the darkness. Then I caught his scent and his heat.

"Seb?"

The bed shifted, and I felt him stretch out next to me.

"Mina." He said my name as a sigh, and as he reached for me, I also caught the faint scent of alcohol. His lips closed over mine and I tasted it, too, the single-malt whisky he preferred, the desperate desire in his kiss.

Or maybe that desperation was mine. I'd missed his touch, and now it seemed his hands were everywhere on my body. My own slid over him, over his naked chest, the boxer shorts that did little to keep his erection from burning me where he pressed against my thigh.

Not quite awake, not quite asleep, sex was a fever dream of sensation, and when he finally slid inside me, we both made little whimpering sounds as if we'd finally been allowed something denied so long.

I came, again and again, the climax fading into sleep where it seemed to keep going forever.

THERE WAS MUSIC playing. Loudly. Irritatingly.

Then my mind pulled together the notes, the familiarity, and I realized it was my phone ringing. I sat up, eyes squinting open, and reached for the cell where it rested on the side table. As I flipped it open, a groan and the creaking of the sofa bed made me look over my shoulder. At Sebastian, naked, pulling the covers over his head. So it hadn't all been a dream.

"Ms. Cavallari?"

"Yes?" My voice was rough and too high, and I coughed, trying to wake myself up.

"It's Roberta Small, dear." Sleepiness turned into excitement. It had been about a month since I'd last talked with her.

"Yes, how are you doing?"

"Did I call too early?" she asked, and then rushed on before I could assure her it wasn't. Not that I knew the time. "I wanted to thank you for putting me in touch with my cousin. Bruce and Sally are just lovely, and their kids as well." I listened to her go on and on about what a lovely family it was and how they planned to have a family picnic this summer if they could gather all the relatives."

I was happy for her, but if that was the entirety of why she was calling me on a Saturday morning at an hour that was too early regardless of what it was in actuality, I could have done without.

"I'm so pleased that worked out for you," I said instead.

"And I wanted to let you know that my cousin Paul in Bedfordshire thinks he has some letters that might interest you."

Excitement thrummed again, and I asked her to hold on while I fumbled for a pen and one of my spiral notebooks. I wrote Paul's name and number down and thanked her. It was entirely possible that this guy had nothing, or that his findings would lead to nowhere in my search for a connection to James Mead, just as with Bruce Mallard's treasure trove. Entirely possible, but I was still blissful from the 2 A.M. sex and the progress I was making in every other aspect of the research. I wanted to be hopeful.

I hung up with her and snuggled back under the covers next to Sebastian. With a small, sleepy growling noise, he wrapped me in his arms. I smiled against his chest. I needed to call Paul, but it could wait just a few more minutes.

SEBASTIAN WAS IMPOSSIBLY sweet to me that day, touching me constantly, looking at me with this indescribable intensity that was very different from the intensity of his desire, and when, a few hours later, I'd arranged to go out to Cranfield the following day, he offered to drive me. Which I, of course, accepted.

So Sunday morning we headed out. Cranfield was in the north of Central Bedfordshire, about thirty minutes past Luton, which itself was an hour outside of London. Of course, back in Anne's day, those minutes would have been hours or even days.

I had been up this way several months ago to see the area and homes in which Anne had spent the majority of her life. I looked in the church records for the marriage and birth records, enjoyed seeing her signature. I had seen the name Randall on the list of local gentry, but there had never been a connection other than proximity before.

Paul Randall lived in his family's ancestral home. Though he was a relation of Roberta Small, he wasn't actually a blood relative of Anne's. Instead, he was a descendant of a contemporary of hers with whom she had exchanged numerous letters.

If I had been more thorough in my research on all of Anne's neighbors, perhaps I would have stumbled upon him earlier.

As it was, we pulled up to a pretty, ivy-covered two-story house that was surrounded by big lavender bushes.

"A cozy cottage," Sebastian observed. Which made me laugh since, to me, four thousand square feet was nearly a mansion. But it was petite compared to the nearby manor house, and the size suggested that Paul's nineteenth-century ancestor had been well-to-do in a "genteel" sort of way.

"Phillip Randall," the slim, fiftysomething man said as he led us through the house, "was a solicitor. Runs in the family," he added with a laugh. "From what I understand, he was against the enclosure act as a young man, then an early champion of labor reform, education reform..."

He brought us into the kitchen, which was bright with sunlight, and where, on a huge farmhouse table, he'd laid out several piles of letters.

"I've been in the process of conducting an inventory

of everything in the house," Paul continued, gesticulating toward the table. "I doubt I ever would have known this existed otherwise, but I'm the last Randall at the moment. Someone needs to do this."

"This is fabulous," I said, resting my hand on the back of one of the chairs. "May I?"

"Go right ahead." I sat down, reaching for one of the stacks, distantly aware that Sebastian sat as well. I was entranced by Anne Gracechurch's writing on the outer fold of the letter. I'd seen quite a bit of her correspondence over the last year and a half, at the Huntington Library in California, at various other archives and literary collections, in the collection of her publisher. Every time, a thrill buoyed me, that here I was bridging the distance between history and the present, fiction and reality. That the mystery of this author previously relegated to obscurity was mine to explore.

"Anne Gracechurch is an author, you say?" Paul asked as I unfolded the first letter carefully. He was leaning against the center island, watching. I had a pair of cotton gloves in my bag and I stopped for a moment to pull them out, to protect the paper from the oils of my skin. Not that the kitchen table was the cleanest of workspaces for archival work to begin with. But while I didn't know what would happen to these letters after I'd left, I didn't want to add to their decay. I hoped that someday a Gracechurch collection could be created and hosted at a university or a museum.

"You haven't read these?" Surely, the answer to his question was clear from her correspondence that she wrote. Every letter I had ever read of hers, other than the domestic ones at the Mallards', had been rife with literary discussions.

"A few only. Mostly political diatribes," he answered with a shrug. That was interesting. I wondered what her relationship with Phillip Randall had been like. I looked at the date on the letter in my hand—1827. Two years before the first James Mead book was published, a morality tale about the dangers of corruption in pocket boroughs. *Coincidence?*

Beyond excited, I pulled out a notebook and pen, as well as my camera, and slid them over to Sebastian. I filled Paul in on Anne's life as I worked, first rearranging the piles by date. He was a lively man who asked insightful questions, and soon he was part of the team, taking over the notebook from Sebastian to copy down my dictation, while Seb took numerous photographs of each letter. Although I'd worked one summer for one of my English professors, I'd never had assistants before, and it was an enjoyable novelty to work in a team.

We broke briefly for lunch, moving to an outside table in the garden for sandwiches before returning inside to finish.

A narrative was developing as I read, and, while I'd have to go back through my notes to verify, I was fairly certain based on the timeline that this relationship with Phillip had been a huge inspiration for Anne's social work and an instigator in the acrimony between her and her husband.

"In these early letters, she keeps referring to Mary and

the poor children," I commented. "Is that his wife?"

"Yes, she died in childbirth according to the family Bible," Paul filled in. "Phillip had two surviving children."

"What year was that?" Sebastian asked. He had that thoughtful look on his face, the one where he looked like he was chewing the inside of his mouth. Paul went to get the Bible and check.

"What are you thinking?"

Seb turned the camera on me and snapped a quick shot even as I held up a hand in front of my face.

"I'm thinking they were lovers."

I rolled my eyes. "Of course it would be about sex."

"No, think about it, Mina. Isn't this just before the James Mead books? And weren't those books at the same time as she was having marital troubles? So she's friends with Phillip's wife, who dies, and in comforting him and the children, they strike up a friendship, intellectual at first, then"—he shot me a hot look that made me squirm on the wooden seat—"as we know, intellectual attraction easily turns into physical."

I twisted my lips, ignoring the suggestion that it was my intelligence that had attracted him to my body when it had been very easy for him to ignore me when sex wasn't on the table. The conjecture about Anne and Phillip was an interesting theory but one I wanted to reject. As I turned back to the last stack of letters, I examined why I felt that way. Was it because I had some idealistic view of the past? Like people from the nineteenth century didn't commit adultery or sleep around or have premarital sex? I knew that wasn't true. But emotionally, was that a false story I still bought into?

Paul returned, and the date supported Sebastian's theory.

"Listen to this!" I exclaimed with excitement, forgetting Sebastian's theory. "She writes, 'I find it harder to write of Caroline and Mayberry'—those were the protagonists of *At Michaelmas*," I inserted. "'When I think of the poor who will never have such an education, will never know what it is to rise above brute labor.'"

I looked at Paul and Sebastian. "Okay, it doesn't quite prove that she wrote about education reform, but it shows she leaned toward it and certainly at the same time as James Mead was about to publish his book fictionalizing the plight of children."

But even as I said it, I knew that it was still not enough. Circumstantial. Considering the milieu of the time, many reformers felt the same, might have done the same. There might very well have been a James Mead who did. Or Randall might have been James Mead. I would have loved an example of Phillip's writing to Anne, but unfortunately those letters were either lost to the past or still hiding somewhere out of my grasp.

Several letters later, I read another snippet aloud: "'I cannot visit again this summer. Mr. Gracechurch returns and wishes to reconcile. For the children's sake.'"

There had been great affection apparent in the other letters, but this was the first that said anything quite so bluntly.

"Do you think they were having an affair?" Paul asked.

I looked at Sebastian, who smirked. My lips twisted again I had to concede. "It's definitely a possibility."

"It's not what you hoped for, but it's not a loss," Sebastian said when we got in the car. I blinked and stared at him. He met my gaze. "I know you're disappointed. It's obvious. No, not to Paul, don't worry, but to me. But this is one of those things that happen. You find useful information, not the information you hoped for. But still useful."

He turned his attention to the road, and so did I, staring at the outline of trees in the twilight. He was right. Not that it helped settle my emotions at all. This whole process was a roller coaster.

"It's like trading, or playing poker," Seb continued. "There are the highs and the lows. Good thing is, there's no real losing for you here. No millions down in a millisecond."

"I still think that's ridiculous," I said, fully distracted now. "That people make a career on gambling. Or on insuring someone's gamble. On real things that other people make. See, *that* I understand. Manufacturing. Creating something."

"From the woman who wants to have a nice, tenured university job where she's insulated from the realities of the economy. Where you'll spend, what? Maybe ten hours a week actually teaching and helping with education and the rest of your time writing grants for more money to help fund your writing about topics that don't actually create anything useful for people."

"Wow, don't hold back or anything."

"I'm exaggerating for effect, Mina," he said with a laugh. "The point is that many jobs don't actually create anything fundamentally necessary. We happen to be lucky enough to spend our time intellectually masturbating, so why shouldn't we embrace it?"

He had a point, even if I was certain I could poke holes in his case if I thought more deeply about it. Regardless, he'd successfully distracted me from a potential funk. Overall, for the dissertation as a whole, today had been a success. The letters added depth to understanding Anne Gracechurch and her milieu. Helped contextualize her seeming obsession with romantic stories, with heroes who were everyday men, not men with £10,000 a year.

I slanted a glance at Sebastian. Not quite a Darcy, but certainly not an everyday man.

And not my hero either.

Chapter Eleven

THE NEXT DAYS were an idyll. We didn't talk about the fight we'd had, or about the silent reconciliation. We simply enjoyed each other. And we worked well together. The trips to Stanton Hall and to Bedfordshire had proven that.

Even more, I didn't want to be sad, or stressed, or worried about my nonexistent relationship. Much better to take it for what it was: hot sex and enjoyable companionship.

He didn't push me to reveal more of myself, and I didn't push him. Yet, somehow, day by day, I did come to understand him, to recognize his moods and his desires.

Research progressed at a faster pace than it had in the spring, and I was grateful that I'd been able to stay these extra months. I reanalyzed Anne's writing in context of the new information I'd gleaned about her life and found that the rough draft of my planned six-chapter dissertation seemed to spill from my fingers. Perhaps I didn't have the James Mead connection yet, but still—whereas last fall I was facing the possibility of having to extend to a sixth year, now I was nearly ahead of the game.

And one week after the trip to Bedfordshire, I made major progress on the Harridan House project as well. I'd managed to narrow down the disparate entries between the two estate books to six, one of which was a payment to Venus & Satyr Art Brokerage, which, with a name like that, was either truly a firm that sold art or a front for Harridan House. Or perhaps both. I wanted to return to Stanton Hall to see how far back that company was mentioned and if there were other receipts. Then I stumbled upon *The Memoirs of the Incomparable Penny Partridge*.

"I found her!" I crowed, slapping the photocopied version of my latest reading down on the coffee table. It was late morning on a Saturday, and I'd been lounging on the sofa reading a photocopy of a rare book I'd stumbled over partly out of my interest in the nineteenth century and partly because a memoir by a London courtesan of the era seemed like it might mention *something* about a secretive sex club.

Sebastian stopped typing. Looked over at me from the kitchen table.

"Jenny Smollett."

"Who?"

"That's the name of our Madame Rouge. Or rather, of the first *named* Madame Rouge. I suspect there was one before her because her age is far too young to have been around when the club first began."

"You're saying Madame Rouge is a position."

"I believe so. Like the pope."

He laughed. "I doubt that the Catholic Church would appreciate that comparison."

"It's only funny or vaguely appropriate because they used to call brothels nunneries."

"That changes everything then. I'm certain the pope would approve."

I rolled my eyes.

"So who was Jenny Smollett?"

"From what I understand based on this courtesan's memoirs, she was a mistress who was cast out of her protector's home for participating in an orgy at Harridan House—or rather, as Penny Partridge puts it, 'that mysterious house of every vice imaginable.' She never actually mentions it by name. Then she showed up again a year later as 'the turbaned madam known as Rouge.'"

"But it's never actually called Harridan House?"

"Sebastian, this is a huge break. It's far too much of an overlap to be coincidental. If I found this sort of connection between Gracechurch and Mead, I'd be set."

He nodded slowly. "How *did* you find this, Mina?"

"Luck." I shrugged. "When I came across her memoirs, I just thought . . . maybe she'd mention something of interest. After all Harriette Wilson let loose lots of brilliant gems about society when she wrote her exposé of England's most powerful men."

He didn't know who Harriette Wilson was, so our conversation turned into a little history lesson about the notorious Regency courtesan who'd counted the Duke of

Wellington, prime ministers, and a whole slew of aristocrats and royals as her clients and then, to support herself in her old age, blackmailed those men with the threat of her memoirs. Wellington had famously said, "Publish and be damned."

Which, she did. Although maybe not damned, since people gobbled up those memoirs like gossip rags.

"Brilliant," Sebastian said, but I wasn't certain if he was commenting on Wilson or on the fact that we'd made progress in understanding Harridan House.

Despite his hesitancy, I was bolder than Sebastian in my research. Not so afraid that my inquiries would somehow reflect back on his family. After all, if I didn't mention his grandfather, there was no logical reason anyone would connect Harridan House to the viscountcy at all.

Now I had a name to research: Jenny Smollett. We still hadn't gone to talk to his great-aunt Rose or the ninety-five-year-old childhood friend of his grandfather's, but, because of his qualms, we were leaving that as a last resort.

I wasn't certain what Sebastian hoped to learn, how extensive a history of the club he desired, but nonetheless, we'd made progress.

Which meant I got a much-deserved day of sightseeing. Days really. We spent the rest of the weekend going to museums and walking hand in hand in parks like the lovers we were. There was no tension, no underlying manipulative subtext on either of our parts.

I refused to think about the future or the past and instead enjoyed the beautiful, endless present.

On Tuesday, I dressed in shorts and a tank top with the intention of taking my laptop with me to St. James's Park and lying out in the sun while I worked.

As I was gathering papers to put in my backpack, my cell rang. The number was withheld.

"Hello?"

"Is this Ms. Cavallari?"

Excitement thrummed through me. I didn't recognize the voice, but I had so many calls out to different people that this woman could be any number of people. If I had to make a guess, I'd say from the slight rasp, that she was fortysomething, or maybe fifty. I sat down on the couch and grabbed my spiral notebook and pen. Perhaps Roberta Small had turned into a dead end, but that didn't mean every lead would.

"I'd like to meet you."

"I'm sorry. Who did you say was calling?" I asked.

"I didn't. Meet me at The Silver Arms, at 12:30 P.M. today. In Camden." The line clicked off.

I stared at my phone, the excitement lessening to a nervous indecision. Why the secrecy? No one with whom I'd left my number should have any need to require anonymity. There was no logical reason for an action that reeked of sinister intention.

It was 10 A.M. I had no idea where the pub was, but with the Internet, directions would be easy, and I knew where Camden was. Vaguely. I'd planned to go shopping at the markets there at some point, but I hadn't yet found the time, even though I was living only two Tube stops away.

A pub was a busy place, and lunch hour the busiest time of all. What harm could there be?

Only all the dangers that tended to befall people in novels and movies.

But it wasn't like she'd said to come alone.

I opened my contacts list and pressed on Seb's name. It went to voice mail.

"It's Mina. I just got a very strange call. Call me back, okay?"

But what if he didn't? What if I went and no one knew where I'd gone and something happened to me?

I'd phone Sebastian again on my way over and tell him exactly where I was going and why. And I wouldn't eat anything at the pub, in case . . .

I shook my head. I'd entered full paranoia mode. This wasn't some spy novel. I was a graduate student doing fairly innocuous research. But the whole private number, no name, quick phone call was decidedly odd. Anyone would think so.

Still. At twelve, I left the flat and walked over to the King's Cross Station, ringing Sebastian up again.

"Mina, I just saw you called." Relief flooded through me at the sound of his voice. I wasn't alone.

"I'm going to a pub two blocks from the Camden Town Tube stop. The Silver Arms. This woman called me from a blocked number and said to meet her there, and she wouldn't say her name. It's weird, right?"

"Exceedingly. Where are you? I'll take lunch now and meet you at the Tube."

"I was hoping you'd say that."

There was a different energy that I noticed the minute I stepped outside the Tube station at Camden. I waited on the sidewalk, watching the crowds of people go by.

I slung my arm back at the touch of hands on my hips.

"Easy." At Sebastian's voice, I relaxed and turned in his arms.

"I thought you were a pickpocket."

He pulled me in close, lowering his head. "Maybe I am . . . and I'm going to steal a kiss."

The line was sort of cheesy, but the kiss was not. I didn't care that it was lunch hour and we were standing on a busy street with people drifting around us as if we were a rock in a river. All that mattered was the delicious heat of his mouth, the way his lips and tongue could awaken every pore of my body so easily.

"All right," he said, breaking away. "Let's find out who this woman is."

The Silver Arms was a relatively quiet restaurant just off Camden High Street. The occupants were in groups of threes and fours, people stepping out from the office for a bite. No one looked mysterious or sinister. No one greeted us or passed us a clandestine note.

So we took a seat and waited. Ordered lunch and waited.

By the time Sebastian had paid the bill, and it was time for him to return to the office, it seemed clear this woman was not going to show. We left the pub and stepped back into the beautiful summer day. It was nice, at least, to have had lunch with Sebastian midweek. Unusual and different.

"Are you certain it was the right number?"

"She called me Miss Cavallari."

"Hmm. What else did she say?"

"Almost nothing. I don't know who she is or what she wanted to meet me about. Now I guess I'll never know.

But later that evening, just after Sebastian returned home, the phone rang again with a withheld number. I answered it cautiously.

"Miss Cavallari, I apologize for not meeting with you this afternoon, but I had to investigate your friend, you understand."

Investigate. What the hell had I gotten myself into here?

"Who are you?"

"I'll answer that later. Suffice to say, you've been asking questions, and I'm willing to give you some answers. Tonight. In thirty minutes a car will arrive to take Mr. Graham and you to meet me. I understand this is all very secretive and rather unusual, but you shall understand the need for discretion once we meet. No harm will come to you."

The call clicked to an end. I put my phone down in disbelief and looked up at Seb, who had stopped halfway across the room, as if he had sensed that this was another call from the mysterious woman.

"She's sending a car to pick us up. To meet with her. So she can give me answers."

"Us? Answers about what? Is one of Gracechurch's descendants part of some mafia?"

I didn't answer that. It was entirely possible for all I knew.

"So we're going to do this, then," he pressed. "Forgo all caution and take this ride?"

I was anxious and unsure. It did sound dangerous, even with Sebastian by my side. But at the same time...

"It's just too strange to let it pass. She did say 'no harm will come to you.' Surely that's something."

He laughed. "Or the fact that she felt the need to mention it could suggest that there are times someone might have to worry."

He was right.

"We don't have to go."

He was silent for a moment, studying me. Then he came close, took me in his arms. "Risk is my world, but this isn't the sort of risk I usually take on. Still, I rather think this is something we'll have to do."

Thirty minutes later, we stood in front of Sebastian's building, and a black sedan pulled up. A man in a black suit stepped out from the backseat and looked at us.

"Miss Cavallari? Mr. Graham?"

At our affirmative nods, he gestured to the backseat. On trembling legs, I approached the car and ducked my head to enter.

A long cardboard box rested on the leather, and I moved it as I slid into the car. The front seat was separated from the back by a smoky glass mirror. Sebastian followed me a moment later. Then the other man slid into the car.

"Inside the box, you will find two blindfolds. Put them on."

I glanced at Seb, who shrugged, and I opened the box. Inside were two long strips of blue silk. And at the edge, embroidered in gold, the letters HH.

I looked back at Sebastian again. He'd lost his cautious calm, his mouth hanging open in astonishment. Our gazes met.

"Seb," I said, lifting one length of silk with reverence even as I voiced what we were both thinking. "It still exists."

Chapter Twelve

I WAS ACUTELY aware of every sound. Of my footsteps on a marble floor. Of the sound of laughter or some sort of party in the distance, the tinkling of glasses, the symphony of male and female voices, muted.

The faint creak of a door opening, accompanied by the breeze made by its passage, and then plush carpet beneath my feet. I struggled not to stumble in my heels on the suddenly softer surface.

I felt knuckles scrape along the back of my head, and then the blindfold was gone. The atmospheric yellow light of the wall sconces was near blinding after the total darkness, and I blinked to adjust.

I looked to my left and saw Sebastian, intent and focused on our surroundings. I wanted to reach for his hand, but that was childish. I felt like Alice through the looking glass, in a world that was both absurd and sinister. One that had heard me whisper its name in libraries, archives, and museums, in conversations with historians. And someone with whom I had conversed, who had expressed no knowledge of this secret world, had passed my name on. Who?

The small room was hard and lush at the same time, with thick carpet over dark hardwood and red wall hangings.

A woman stepped in front of us, a mocking little smile on her face, and she gestured to the room in general.

"Welcome to Harridan House."

Despite that raspy voice that had made me think she was close to fifty, she appeared a decade or so younger. She sported sleek red hair caught up in a French twist. A leather half mask of the sort one might see in Venice during Carnivale obscured her face.

In her hand were another two strips of black silk. She handed one to each of us.

"I am Rouge."

Rouge. Like *Madame Rouge*. Now that was interesting. "There are rules here at Harridan House, and as guests, you must obey those and more. These masks are to protect your identity. Some members forgo masks entirely, and some prefer more substantive ones." She gestured to her own face. "Or even full masks that obscure the shape of the mouth. Secrecy and discretion are paramount even if you do recognize someone despite his/her disguise. We do not discuss the club outside its walls."

"Do we sign a nondisclosure agreement or something like that?" I asked. My voice was a shock even to me in the decadence of this little room.

She laughed. "Utterly unnecessary. If you talked about it, the damage would already be done. Suing you would be of no purpose."

I glanced at Sebastian out of the corner of my eye. His entire body was tense although he was doing a wonderful job of pretending to look nonchalant about the undertones of what Rouge was saying.

"I see you both understand." Her gaze flitted back and forth between the two of us, and then she nodded with a smirk before continuing. "As I said, secrecy and discretion are paramount. Anything you do here at Harridan House will remain in confidence. However, guests are not allowed to participate in any exchange of body fluids, or to engage in intercourse, even with rubbers. Members and employees must undergo monthly exams to ensure that they pass all health requirements. Naturally, nothing is foolproof. If you choose to join after tonight, you will have only guest privileges until you pass your first physical."

I listened to this recitation with both awe and trepidation. Tonight would likely be the only night I ever visited Harridan House and I was absolutely fascinated. I'd taken one anthropology course as an undergrad, and I knew some anthro PhD would kill for the chance to study a subculture such as this one, completely shrouded in secrecy.

"The dress code. Most members choose to wear the black cloak only, allowing for freer physical access. Some prefer to wear evening gowns and black tie. No casual clothing is allowed." Her gaze swept down our bodies.

Sebastian was in his work suit, and I was in a casual summer dress, nothing remotely black tie. "When we have finished our discussion, I will lead you to the changing rooms. Do you have any questions?"

Any? I had dozens of questions.

"How did you become Madame Rouge?"

I glanced over at Sebastian, somewhat surprised though I shouldn't have been. He knew everything I did about the history of Harridan House, which wasn't all that much. And we definitely didn't know its story since 1944.

Rouge was silent for a moment.

"You realize, of course, Mr. Graham, that we conducted an extensive investigation into your background, as we do with all prospective members. You, as well, Miss Cavallari."

"Under normal circumstances, Mr. Graham, you would not have come to our attention until . . . perhaps . . . you'd made greater strides in your career. But we've confirmed that your grandfather was in fact a member of the club in its prior incarnation. And we confirmed from a number of your ex-girlfriends, or perhaps I should say ex-lovers, that you are indeed the sort of man who would contribute to the greater pleasure."

Rouge's gaze swung to me. "You, Miss Cavallari, would never have come to our attention."

I flushed. How much had she actually been able to dig up on me? Which one-night stands and random hookups had she managed to track down?

"Our?" Sebastian prodded, even though she hadn't

answered his last question and, I suspected, she had no intention of revealing any information other than what she initiated.

"The club," she said, which was a vague enough answer as to say nothing. "Now, time for your tour."

DESPITE THE HEAVY black cloak that warded off any possible chill, I was acutely aware of my nakedness. And likely that was why Rouge had insisted we dress this way for our tour. I overlapped the edges and clutched the fabric tightly closed as I stepped out into the hall. Sebastian was already waiting for me in the empty hall, and I giggled at the sight of him in his cloak and mask. How was this sexy?

His lips quirked up, but he didn't laugh. "It's rather unfair that you find me ridiculous, and I find you impossibly sexy." He stepped forward, reaching for me. "Maybe that's because I know what's beneath this shroud." He pushed my hands away and slipped his own between the folds. It didn't matter that anyone could walk in, that likely Rouge would any moment. His hands on my bare hips encompassed my entire world, and I swayed toward him.

"We're here, Mina," he rasped against my cheek. "We've found it. And I would like nothing better than to fuck you here right now."

"That will have to wait." Rouge's voice cut through our little world, and I stepped away from Sebastian, swiftly pulling my cloak together.

"Does the prohibition against intercourse apply to us?" Sebastian demanded, a hint of laughter in his voice.

Rouge cocked her head to the side thoughtfully. "I don't have all night to chaperone you. Follow me." She turned and headed down the hallway.

Again, no direct answer to our questions. But we followed anyway. After all, this was why we were here.

We passed through a warren of hallways, and every so often, the hint of voices, laughter, suggestive moans, would waft through the air toward us. There were no windows anywhere, and I was beginning to get the sense that we were literally underground.

It was a weekday, yet there were all these people in nooks and crannies, satisfying their basest desires. We stopped at an open door and peered inside. I inhaled sharply at the starkness of the activity within. A woman, nude, lay bent over a rounded, padded bar, like the kind I'd seen used at the gym for lower-back strengthening, her large breasts squashed against the vinyl. Behind her was a man, equally nude, strikingly muscular, hand gripping her hips as he fucked her. The slick, wet sound of their coupling and the scent of their efforts and desire were overwhelming.

Were they strangers? The thought disgusted me at the same time that heat grew heavy between my legs. Not that I should judge, considering my past history. But then . . . I judged myself as well.

The next room we passed by had a different configuration—two men and a woman—and it was the first time I'd ever seen anal sex outside of erotica. Even the porn movie I'd seen hadn't had anything like that.

Seeing that much real sex happening in front of me was shocking. Strange. There was both an immense power and a terrible vulnerability to all these naked bodies. Beautiful and horrifying and arousing all at once.

I wanted to hold Sebastian's hand, but we passed through the club on our separate journeys. I had no idea if he saw our surroundings with a critic's eye or if it was everything he had ever imagined it to be.

"This is the lounge," Rouge said as we stepped into a larger space with a checkered marble floor.

There was a bar and tables, and a handful of people were eating and drinking, chatting as if this were any other club.

How did a place like this exist and avoid the attention of the government, of regulations? Or maybe it was known. Maybe among a certain set, Harridan House was an open secret. Maybe bribes were made and eyes averted, or whoever was in charge of licensing was as into swinging and orgies as the rest of the club members.

I didn't know, and Rouge was not exactly a fount of information. I was beginning to realize that she—and her secret partners—had decided it was safer having us more knowledgeable and managed by the threat of death than researching on our own, free to publish and publicize. Not that that had ever been the plan.

Maybe thirty people filled the room, and this just on a Tuesday night. How filled would it be come the weekend?

And who were these people?

"This is the playroom," Rouge announced, when we

stopped at the threshold of another cavernous room. It looked like what I'd always imagined a BDSM dungeon to look like, filled with toys and contraptions that might also be found in a sixteenth-century torture chamber. Although perhaps a little more hygienic and vinyl-covered than splintered wood and rusted spokes. The room was currently empty.

"Popular space," I commented, hoping to draw *something* out of our hostess.

"Everyone has their kink," she said simply. "This isn't yours."

I wasn't certain how she gathered that from my small comment, but I was pretty certain she was right. Despite the little showdown Seb and I had had a few weeks earlier in which he'd claimed I was a secret submissive, pain and serious bondage weren't exactly high on my list. Or even on the list at all.

We passed by another closed door with the unmistakable sounds of sex emanating from within. I was starting to understand the unspoken codes: closed door meant privacy requested, open door meant feel free to watch. We stepped into the next open room, which was empty. But Rouge walked over to the wall and pulled the draperies aside, revealing a window into the closed room next door.

And suddenly I was watching one man give another man a blow job.

"I thought the closed door meant privacy," I choked out, my gaze never leaving the exhibition before me.

"It means do not disturb, do not join," Rouge corrected. "But there is always a way to watch, and that is understood."

Do not join. I imagined that, walking into a room where two people were already having sex and simply adding my body to the mix. How did anyone know if they were really welcome or desired? Or did that matter here? Was every body interchangeable?

I glanced over at Sebastian. He, too, was watching the men. I wondered if it turned him on.

Rouge drew the curtain shut. She shot me an amused glance as she passed me on the way out of the room. "That isn't his."

I blinked, then followed her, Sebastian a step behind. His hand brushed against me, pushing the voluminous folds of cloth against my backside. I looked back at him and shivered at the intensity of his gaze. This tour, combined with that look in his eyes, was possibly the most torturous foreplay in the world.

Another open door and inside a bed with three occupants. In my head I heard the documentary announcer: *And here we see another common phenomenon amongst these underground mammals. Watch the female cohabit with two males, an evolutionary adaptation as a result of lack of resources.*

I snickered at my thoughts, and Rouge sent me a seething glare. Right.

But it was just too much. I was getting overwhelmed with all the different permutations and combinations. I wanted to go back to Sebastian's flat and feel him inside me with plain old one-on-one sex. Somehow Harridan House had been more erotic as a mystery set in the past, created solely in my imagination.

The rest of the tour passed by in a blur of naked, thrusting bodies. I noticed the glass bowls of assorted condoms strategically placed throughout, as well as bottles of lube and clean, folded towels, like this was a spa.

Of course, there was an actual spa as well, shower rooms, a sauna, hot tub.

The tour wound up back at the changing rooms where we had first shed our clothes in favor of the cloaks.

"Change," Rouge commanded, "and I'll see you back in the office."

She left us in front of our respective dressing rooms. I opened the door and was startled when Sebastian pushed me forward, his body crowding mine as he shut the door behind him. I turned to face him, every fiber of my body awake to his desire. We'd both been on edge as we'd watched the panoply of erotic scenes.

"I've been sporting a painful hard-on all night," Sebastian said, holding up a little foil square that he'd clearly lifted from one of the many convenient, expensive crystal bowls, and ripped it open. I watched him push his cloak to the side, revealing his pale, nude body and clear arousal. He slid the condom down his length and then reached for me, under my cloak, grabbing my backside and pulling me close. "And conveniently . . ."

He lifted me, and my legs slipped around his hips, pushing the voluminous fabric of his cloak aside. My sex nestled against him, and with that contact, I could feel how damp I was. Then he hoisted me up a bit more and brought me back down as he thrust up.

I cried out at the sudden, piercing pleasure of it, even as he pushed me against the wall of the changing room. How many others had stood here in this same way, unable to hold back? Sebastian's groan pulled me back from clear thought, and I slid my hands down his arms, reveling in his lean strength.

"Mina," he gasped into my ear as his hips pistoned against mine in an increasingly frantic rhythm. "I could fuck you forever."

The way he said my name made the vulgar words sound tender and meaningful. Like no other woman would have satisfied him.

"Do it," I whispered, closing my mouth over the smooth skin of his neck before the movement of his body sent my head back against the wall again. At that moment, sex wasn't about finding my way to orgasm. Instead, I enjoyed the power of this male body inside me and around me. Every sound he made, every hint that he was nearing his crisis, gave me intense pleasure that had little to do with my clitoris or any of the myriad nerve endings on fire in my body.

He stiffened, pushed up into me hard, my breasts flattened against his chest, and I wrapped myself even more tightly around him as he shuddered, hips still moving but more slowly now.

Finally, he pulled out and held me until I was steady

on my feet, his forehead pressed against mine. "Thank you," he whispered.

I let out a breathy laugh. He took my face in his hands and kissed me lightly on the lips.

"Thank you for finding Harridan House. For being here. For sharing your body with me. For everything."

I didn't know what to say to that. *You're welcome* hardly seemed appropriate. But he didn't seem to expect a response. Instead, he slid down my body, his mouth finding my right breast, closing over the nipple, and I sighed at the sweet sensation of that touch.

TEN MINUTES OR so later, we found our way back to the office.

Rouge glanced over us. A small smirk twisted her lips. "I see you've enjoyed your visit to our little club." Two blindfolds lay prominently on the desk. We'd be leaving the way we'd arrived, in secrecy. "Will we be seeing you again?"

This unworldly moment, hidden underground in a secret sex club, this wasn't part of regular life. Certainly not mine. But Sebastian? Was this what he wanted?

I looked over to him and found him watching me. Then he turned back to Rouge decisively. "Yes."

"Excellent," Rouge said. "I'll be in touch. Thomas will see you home." She rounded the desk and picked up the blindfolds. I watched her tie the cloth over Sebastian's eyes first. Watching her touch him emphasized clearly that this was the beginning of the end. I'd been staying at Sebastian's for maybe six weeks, but it felt like far more. Like an eternity, and I had six weeks before I was scheduled to go home. But now he was planning to return to Harridan House. And he wouldn't just be an observer.

Which... unsettled me.

I didn't have any sort of claim over him, nor did I want one, but it did mean that our little affair might end earlier than I had anticipated.

Rouge turned to me. I was shorter than her, even in my heels, so she didn't need to reach up like she had with Sebastian. The cool silk settled over my eyes, turning the world dark, and then I felt her fingers brushing against my hair, the sensitive skin of my scalp, as she tied it firmly. Her fingers brushed down over my neck, my arm, and then her touch and her scent were gone.

Chapter Thirteen

BACK AT SEBASTIAN's apartment, we sat on the sofa and stared at each other.

"So that was . . . interesting," I said with a nervous laugh.

Sebastian stared at me. "Compelling, rather. And to think it's been here all these years. Even my grandfather didn't know."

"Perhaps it was revived only recently." But even as I suggested it, I knew it didn't entirely make sense because that would have meant that people knew the history and had decided, all these years later, to begin the club anew.

"Perhaps," Sebastian said, noncommittal.

"Not that it exists even now," I said, opting for a more lighthearted approach. We couldn't speak of the place on pain of death, at least, that was the gist of Rouge's unspoken threat.

"All these years the conspiracy theorists worried

about Bilderberg . . . And forget deals forged over a golf course. Did you see who was there tonight?"

I tried to remember, but all I saw was a sea of masked faces. Would I have recognized anyone even if their faces were as bare as their naked bodies? I shook my head.

"These are the power brokers, Mina." His eyes were alight with excitement, and I knew that the idea turned him on as much as the sexual acts we had witnessed. "It isn't the same as the club grandfather frequented. This isn't just the playground of the bored and aimless nobleman. Not by a long shot. No wonder it's so secretive. No wonder we were brought into the fold."

Because it was easier to control us and to control what information was released.

"Amazing that it managed to remain underground all these years."

"Amazing," I repeated. But inside, I felt unsettled. Sebastian was thrilled, but I was confused, unsure of who I was and what I was doing. Harridan House had been like a mirror in a fun house, reflecting my past actions but distorted, writ large. It was one thing to read about a place like that but another entirely to experience it. To have sex in a changing room on the premises.

The funk stayed with me late into the next day. And when, just after dinner, Sebastian announced, "The doctor is coming tomorrow night," I was painfully aware of the schism.

This was real. Sebastian was joining, taking the next step. "Oh," I said simply.

"What? Do you have a fear of needles?"

I stared at him, trying to make sense of what he was saying.

"I told Rouge that we were joining." He emphasized the word *we*.

"But I'm not." I couldn't go back there. If I did, I'd lose any sense of who I was. It would be a mistake. A mistake like all the other mistakes I'd made in the past two years. Like Sebastian was a mistake. How could I have thought him a sign that my life was changing again, turning back? I struggled for something else to say. "I could never afford it."

"Mina, I want you on this journey with me. I'm willing to pay for that. I'm single. I don't have outrageous expenses. I can afford this."

He was going to pay tens of thousands of dollars for us each to belong to a sex club. I wouldn't even be here more than a few weeks. It was hedonistic and wrong.

I shook my head, tension rising inside me, making it difficult for me to stay in one place, sit still in that chair. I'd put myself in a terrible situation. Of course Sebastian thought I'd be up to join him in this. I hadn't given him any other impression. I'd fucked when he wanted to fuck. Dropped to my knees and sucked him off at his slightest command. I was malleable and easy.

He studied me silently. I pressed my lips together hard, struggling not to say all the things pressed up against my mouth. Not to accuse him of still ruining my life.

"It's not right." But I knew I shouldn't have spoken the minute I did.

"What's not right? You had fun tonight. I saw you. You were as turned on as I was."

"It's sybaritic. Debauched."

He frowned. "There's nothing wrong with sex between consenting adults. Nothing wrong with the sex we have. It's not like we have to have sex with other people."

I stood. Looked around the room. My things were everywhere, but I needed to grab it all and get away. I started for my backpack and my research first. But I'd accumulated so much stuff I'd need another suitcase to take it all home.

"What are you doing?"

"Leaving."

He was next to me, his hand on my arm. I shrugged it off.

"Don't be ridiculous. It's the middle of the night. There's nowhere to go."

"I don't care. I can't stay here. Ever since I met you, everything's been fucked up."

That shut him up, and I pushed my stuff into bags as fast as I could. Everything *had* been fucked up.

"What do you mean?" he said finally, the words slow, his tone serious.

Oh God, he wanted me to explain. Of course he did. He'd been pushing for this for weeks. What makes Mina tick? What made Mina turn from naive girl he wouldn't touch with a ten-foot pole into a woman who would want a one-night stand? I was a mystery to him the way Harridan House was. A temporary obsession.

Well, fuck him and his obsessions. I stalked into the

bedroom, pulling the few items I had from the drawer he'd cleared for me. He followed me, filling the room with his overwhelming presence, which angered me more.

"I mean I'm going to go to a hotel. Or a hostel or something. I can't stay here, and I can't go to that club again."

"Forget the club," he said. "This isn't just about that. What did you mean?"

I filled my duffel with clothes and dragged it out of the room to the door, depositing it next to my stuffed backpack and the overflowing shopping bag.

"Be reasonable. If you still want to leave in the morning that's one thing, but you can't leave now. Mina, talk to me."

I looked for my purse, which had my cell phone inside. I needed to find a place to stay, but maybe the doorman at the desk downstairs could help with that. I didn't dare look at Sebastian as I swung my backpack over my arm.

"Mina!" And then silence.

I lifted the shopping bag, holding it on my hip with one hand because it was very likely to break under the weight if I tried to use the handles.

"Mina, take your clothes off."

Even through my fury, I heard those words and that commanding tone of voice, and they made me stop in place.

"What did you say?" I asked slowly, turning to face him, trying to direct my fury to this but stunned and failing. Instead, it was all caught inside me. I was trembling and hot. And wanting him.

"Even with you going nuts, I want to fuck you. Maybe I want to fuck you more."

"Are you saying I'm crazy?" I dropped the shopping bag. Heard it rip with an internal wince.

"I meant you are acting crazy right now." He sighed, running his hand through his hair in a gesture I knew so well. "You aren't going anywhere and you know it. So take your clothes off and let me fuck you." Stupidly, unreasonably, I wanted to do that. Give in to his desires and forget who I was. So much easier. He stepped closer to me. "The way you want. Unashamed of wanting it."

Unashamed.

I was ashamed. The girl who grew up on Austen and Brontë, on Burney and Gaskell, on almost puritanical values despite living in a relatively secular household. I'd spent most of my life obsessed with the nineteenth century and its social mores. Not that it had stopped me from having sex at twenty, but I'd still judged everything.

I stood there, practically shaking with the intensity of my emotions, and yet, I couldn't speak. All the anger, the frustration, self-loathing, and despair were trapped inside.

There was that night after Sebastian had graduated that I'd had my first one-night stand, a political-science grad student who'd been more than happy to come back to my apartment. I'd enjoyed the look on Tanya's face when we'd strutted past her across the living room, the guy's hands all over my body. I hadn't so much enjoyed the next morning. Staring at myself in the mirror, not knowing who I was.

From that moment on, I was unmoored and desperately trying to find my way. Men seemed to sense that I was open to suggestion, and they flocked to me. Knowing I could attract them, attract nearly anyone I wanted but the one person who was no longer in the vicinity, I started taking care of my appearance, molding myself into some other version of Mina—one I didn't know. The first time I plucked my eyebrows was nearly as shocking as sex because the face that stared back at me in that immovable mirror looked different from before. Each time I went out with a new guy, it was as if there would be answers there, some clue to who I was or should be. And yet . . . it was exactly the reverse.

I'd lost myself in increments until the day I'd woken up in some stranger's bed, hungover, just beginning to recall how bad sex had actually been as I stared blearily at the number on my phone. My advisor. Who wanted to know why I'd missed our appointment.

Which wasn't the only important thing I'd missed.

I'd thought that my lowest point.

Now here I was, fucking Sebastian in a sex club's changing room, watching other people have sex and gratify their deviant sexual desires. The little affair that I'd decided would be a fitting end to my tangent was not over. Maybe the tangent was not over.

I was making another mistake.

"Stop thinking," he demanded, and he grabbed my chin, forcing me to look at him. "Or tell me."

"Tell you what?" I bit the words out, glaring at him.

He stared at me hard. Then he let go of me, pulled his

loosened tie free of his collar. He took my wrist and lifted it over my head.

"What are you doing?" I asked, panicked, and yet I didn't move, let him slide the backpack off my shoulder and take my other wrist in his hand.

"What do you think I'm doing?"

He was tying me up.

"Fuck you," I whispered. But something flickered inside me. I was both terrified and soothed. I couldn't leave, even if I wanted to.

"What the hell is the point of this?" I looked up at the ceiling, teeth chattering. "You think *I'm* insane?"

My eyes stung with tears.

He lifted me in his arms and carried me into the bedroom, and with each step he took, my tears came harder. He laid me on the bed and stretched out next to me.

"Mina, what happened?" He pulled me into his arms.

"You. *You* happened," I said bitterly, kicking at him. He shifted to rest his leg over mine and, finally, fully trapped, I burst into tears.

Then I told him. Every embarrassing little detail of my dark ages, from the very first night to the men I barely remembered, to the self-disgust I felt. Through it all, he stroked my hair, my cheek–listened without saying a word. When I was done, he held me in silence. I didn't know what he thought of it, but I almost didn't care. The worst he could do was think I was crazy, as he had said earlier. And so what if he did? I was leaving anyway. He'd wanted to know what was inside my twisted little brain, and now he knew. He knew I blamed him.

"Mina," he said finally, "I feel like I should apologize again, but I can't. We're not static people. We evolve, become more the people we *want* to be. We can't know what would have happened, or if *we* would have happened. So maybe the pendulum swung for you a little too far for comfort, but here you are now, and you're perfect."

"Perfectly broken," I returned sullenly. "I have no ideals anymore."

"Stop feeling sorry for yourself," he said, his hands moving to my shoulders, pushing me away so that he could look me in the face. "That's called growing up. Maybe those weren't the right ideals to have."

I blinked.

With a sigh, he untied my hands.

"Come on, let's get ready for bed and get some sleep. We can talk about this in the morning."

I followed him into the bathroom, where I'd forgotten to pack my toiletries. Silently, I brushed my teeth and washed my face. Then I stripped down to my tank top and underwear and climbed into the bed. As I huddled on the far edge, his words ricocheted through my head. Maybe he was right. Right about all of it.

Maybe it was time to own my actions.

I WOKE TO bright daylight sneaking through the cracks in the draperies. I stretched and snuggled into the mattress, holding tight to the lingering pleasure of sleep. The sound of the shower turning off, the flow of water through the pipes shifting, and Sebastian's footsteps in the bathroom brought me full out of dream into consciousness.

I turned my head into the pillow and squeezed my face against the memory of all that had happened the night before. But I hadn't forgotten the lesson learned: *time to own my actions*. And not just in a "deny and return to some golden era of the past" sort of way.

I was a twenty-six-year-old woman forging a life for herself. I could handle this. I didn't need to run away.

So what did I *really* want?

To stay here with Sebastian until I had to return to the States? Accept the unconditional enjoyment of each other's bodies?

Yes.

Okay then. What about the rest? What about his membership in Harridan House and the one he wanted to get me?

It was his choice what he did with his money, where he ventured, whom he fucked. Though knowing he was at Harridan House, walking through those deep underground corridors, would have a potential impact on my physical relationship with him. I couldn't imagine being okay with that. Not for a week. Not for a month or a summer.

So would I join him?

Jealousy was not a good enough reason to do so.

So what was?

Wait. Was I looking for reasons to accept his offer now? Did I *want* to go back to Harridan House?

I felt the air shift in the room before he even made

any noises, like opening the dresser drawer or draping his towel on the other edge of the bed.

I flipped over in bed to face him and lifted myself up on one arm. He was beautiful in the thin light, that strong, tall, naked body. I loved that body. I wanted to kiss it, lick it, suck it, fuck it.

I wanted to do that here in his flat or out on the streets of London. Or in some decadent club that allowed me to be a voyeur to all the daring sexual acts in which I didn't *actually* want to engage. And he'd said we didn't have to sleep with other people. Maybe, for these last few weeks of my time in London, he'd be satisfied with that.

His gaze met mine. He dropped the underwear he had plucked up, sat down on the edge of the bed, and reached for the outline of my leg under the covers.

"How are you feeling?"

"Good," I said firmly, and it was true. I'd told him everything. I had no secrets and no deception.

He nodded, his hand moving slightly down my calf but then stopping. "Will you stay?"

"I think so. Yes."

He nodded again. "I should get dressed. Get to work."

I glanced at the clock. Nearly eight. Later than his usual routine.

But he didn't move. His jaw worked as if he wanted to say something. I waited. I could make it easier on him, but I wanted to know what went on in that brain of his.

"We should talk more, but I have to go. Tonight?" His forehead was lined with concern. Worried about me or worried about how crazy I was? About the fact that I'd blamed him.

I sat up, climbed over the covers, and crawled over to him. Encircled him with my arms even as my mouth found the tip of his earlobe.

"We can talk, Seb, but we don't need to. You were right yesterday. I need to grow up. So if the offer still stands—"

"You don't need to—"

"—then the answer is yes to Harridan House," I continued, cutting him off. Yes to Sebastian. Yes to my sexual desires. Yes to embracing all of me, even the darkest parts that scared me most.

Yes was my new mantra.

Chapter Fourteen

HARRIDAN HOUSE BECAME our evening amusement. One week after our medical exams, a package was hand-delivered to Sebastian's flat: a velvet box with two masks, an old-fashioned brass key, and the name of a twenty-four-hour liquor store, which we discovered was a front for one of the entrances to the club.

More than one night each week we strolled through its room, indulging our voyeuristic tendencies, and in my case at least, expanding my understanding of the diverse expressions of human sexuality. We wandered in a state of constant arousal, punctuated by release, by Sebastian pulling me into a vacant room, or touching me intimately in an empty corridor. Mostly the club was foreplay, and it charged all the rest of our sexual encounters.

One night, I sat in the lounge, sipping on my champagne with muddled raspberries, waiting for Sebastian to return with another round. There were maybe a half dozen other people in here, drinking, chatting. But the room was well designed, and sound was muted, conversation impossible to overhear. A gleam of light on red hair caught my attention.

Unlike myself, she was wearing a stunning evening gown of black sequins. She could have been walking the red carpet in that outfit while the majority of the rest of us sat here nude or draped in black cloth.

I hadn't seen Madame Rouge since that first night, and I was curious what her role in the club was. According to Sebastian's grandfather, the Madame Rouge of his day had been the owner of the club, as far as he knew, and there had been one memorable entry in which he'd slept with her.

According to Penny Partridge's memoirs, the Madame Rouge before Jenny Smollett took her place was mysterious and only infrequently took men of the club to her bed. Just often enough to make all the men think they had a chance. Smollett, in comparison, was a regular participant in the daily revels.

Likely the change in behaviors affected the tone of Harridan House. Certainly, this current incarnation had a very secretive, darkly seductive feel. The people who frequented the club took their pleasure seriously.

Rouge crossed the room . . . toward me. Slipped into the chair that Sebastian had vacated only moments ago.

"Enjoying yourself?" she asked. The bartender placed a drink in front of her in a well-practiced manner. Clearly, he knew her preferences.

Was I enjoying myself? Somewhat. In a purely

participant-observer sort of way. Not even so much a participant. This wasn't my preference, but as Sebastian had paid my exorbitant membership fee and fairly dared me to cross the Styx with him, here I was. Determined to embrace my sexual desires and refuse guilt. The champagne, too, was delicious.

"It's fascinating," I said. "But what would interest me more is to know what happened between WWII and today."

Rouge laughed. "Such an academic."

I leaned forward slightly. "Yes, I am."

"Am I interrupting?" We both looked up at Sebastian. I'd grown used to him in the mask and cloak and now even found the look a bit dashing, in a masquerade sort of way.

"We were just discussing the history of Harridan House," Rouge said, surprising me. She gestured to a nearby chair, and Sebastian pulled it over, reclaiming his scotch.

"Excellent."

She looked at him, her interest obvious in her gaze. Jealousy seared through me. "You asked how I became Rouge. I'm interested to know how you knew there were many Rouges."

"That was one of the few things we did know," Sebastian said, the slight crease in his forehead making it apparent to me that he thought the question not particularly astute. "My grandfather's journals described Madame Rouge as a woman of some thirty years and . . ." His gaze raked over her boldly. "Unless you've joined the ranks of the undead, I don't believe you to be over a hundred years of age."

I laughed. She didn't.

"I became Rouge seven years ago. I'd been a member for twelve years before that." If she'd been eighteen when she joined, that would make her thirty-seven now. I knew Sebastian was making the same calculations. Likely, Rouge knew that too. "Before me . . . it was more complicated." Her gaze swung back to me. "I learned about the club's history from some of its older members. One gentleman had been coming since puberty. He was quite advanced in years when I met him, the last of the old aristocratic guard. Rouge was quite elderly as well, although she wasn't the Rouge who circulated the club. That was a much younger woman who'd been hired to keep the mystery. For over two hundred years, Harridan House has been owned by women, passed down to women, and now it's mine."

"And why you? How did it become yours?"

The story was vague, but my mind filled in pieces like it was a novel. The man who'd first brought her there was exceedingly wealthy, much older. When their affair had stopped, she'd already met another man at Harridan House, who continued to fund her membership.

She smiled at me as if to say, see, your situation is not so unusual. I flushed because, if our lives were parallel, that made me Sebastian's mistress. I stole a look over at him, discomfort and denial warring with a strange acceptance in my gut.

Maybe I was, living in his home, sleeping in his bed, coming to this club.

"Rouge liked me," she was saying. "She knew everything about everyone who was a member or a guest, and she knew . . . I was the right person to take over when she retired."

"What happened to the other Rouge?" I asked. "The younger one?" It was a bit disorienting, calling all of them by Rouge.

"She was a puppet. That was all she was good for. When Rouge passed away, she left this place to me. I sent the other woman away."

There was something sinister about the matter-of-fact tone in which she said that, and I wondered what "away" meant. Not that I couldn't guess. Her threat to our lives if we did not maintain the club's secrecy had been barely veiled.

"What about before the war?" I asked, shifting the topic slightly to something more comfortable. "I know about the early days." My research into Harridan House's past had slowed since we'd learned of its continued existence. Sebastian's curiosity had seemed mostly satisfied, and we had never discussed the limits of the project. But I was still curious; there was so much history between Jenny Smollett's ascent to the role of Madame Rouge and WWII.

"There is a particular firm that has represented Harridan House for the last 220 years. I never asked about the specifics of this club's origins, but I suspect it is in their records. You have piqued my interest, Miss Cavallari. I assure you that soon I *will* know."

My interest was piqued. I studied literature, not history, but that distinction hardly mattered to my curiosity. I wanted to know the entire biography of this place.

"I . . . We" I amended with a glance at Sebastian, "would be fascinated to know as well."

Rouge's laugh settled into a confident smirk. "Perhaps. But for now, my dear academics, I shall leave you to your pleasure." She leaned forward, reaching out, her fingers stroking the line of my jaw. I flinched in surprise, and she laughed again.

"Such soft skin."

She left silence in her wake. Sebastian lifted his glass and drained the rest, while her touch lingered on my skin. It hadn't been sexual. Rather . . . proprietary. Territorial. As if . . . she *owned* us.

IT WAS STRANGE to spend the days in the normal world and nights in the underground realm of Harridan House. I was intensely aware that I could run into another member of Harridan House and not recognize him or her in street attire. Nude, in a mask, however, I was starting to remember a dozen or so of the club's denizens. Not that the wealthy members likely frequented any of the places I visited, from archives to coffee shops.

It was even more disconcerting to be unable to talk about the experience. For me, everyone but Sebastian became the other. Even Sophie.

Those weekly conversations with Sophie grounded me. She was ambitious and focused on the future, and she wasn't too secretive about her hope that I ended up with a position in New York so that we could finally live in the same city after all these years. She was realistic too. Mentioned all the other careers where my degree and skill set would be useful. Some of which were considerably more lucrative than an academic career.

I appreciated the advice, to a degree. Giving up on academia at this point was tantamount to giving up on finding the link between Anne Gracechurch and James Mead, although, thankfully, the reverse was not true.

But it was difficult to focus on the realities of the future and the job search on which I'd have to embark starting this fall, when the present was so intense and all-consuming.

Toward the latter half of July, we had dinner with Nigel and his fiancée. There were paparazzi outside the restaurant. One of them greeted Sebastian by name but didn't make any attempt to photograph him, reminding me just how much a part of this other world he was even if I had first met him on a university campus. I wondered if the photographers were all for Kate or if there were other celebrities inside. She certainly could easily command this type of attention. I'd seen speculation about her relationship with Nigel in the tabloids. Kate Grinnell, despite not admitting to a thing, was on bump watch. I was anxious about the entire encounter.

Sebastian thought my nervousness hilarious, considering I'd spent the last weeks in the company of ridiculously wealthy and often famous people who were completely nude. But I didn't know or recognize most of the members of Harridan House. For the most part, they weren't famous in a cover of any magazine but *Forbes* sort of a way.

Anyway, this was different. Especially since the last time I'd met Nigel had been that night at his club, when he hadn't been particularly friendly or respectful to me. And this time, there'd be Kate.

They were waiting for us at the bar. Nigel clasped my hands as Kate gave Sebastian an enthusiastic hug. Then Kate and I were introduced. If she was wearing makeup, it was makeup designed to look as if she was wearing none. No image-manipulation magic was necessary to make her look beautiful.

"Such a pleasure to meet you, Mina," she said warmly, even as the hostess appeared to show us to our table. I followed a step behind Kate, who was wearing a flowing silk dress that clung to her body when she moved and if, at nearly five months pregnant, she was showing at all, I couldn't see it.

After we'd all taken our seats, we chatted about the upcoming August wedding, which I'd miss since I would have to return to the States a week earlier. Then conversation flitted from topic to topic, interspersed by the placing our orders and then by the appetizers arriving.

It was shortly after we'd all polished off the calamari and plate of deep fried shishito peppers that Nigel and Sebastian delved into a discussion of one of Nigel's newest ventures, and Kate and I were left with a brief, awkward silence.

"How did you meet Nigel?" I said into the void. It seemed like a safe enough question. Avoided any crazy embarrassment involved in talking with a movie star, someone whose face was so familiar to me and yet who was herself a stranger.

"I've known Nigel for years. He's thirteen years older than me, you know." Which meant she was a year younger than me "I was eighteen, and he just gave me this absolutely smoldering look that is actually how he looks at every new woman he meets." I thought about the way he'd studied me at the club when we'd first met. Not smoldering, but he definitely had laid on the sexual charm instantly. "I had a terrible crush on him, but he practically ignored me. Which was just as well since everyone but me knew he wasn't the sort of man a girl brings home. I figured out fairly quickly that he had cut a swath through half my acquaintances."

"Sounds like Seb," I said.

She laughed and gave me a conspiratorial look. "Admittedly, the stories about those two, not to mention Lydia, Nigel's sister, are rather colorful, but Nigel's changed." She sounded as if she believed that, and I wondered which perspective, Seb's doubts or her faith, would prove to be accurate. "And if *he* can change," Kate continued, "then surely there's hope for Seb yet."

"Oh, I don't need him to change," I denied quickly. "This is sort of a summer fling. Convenient, you could say."

"Hmm." She studied me over her wineglass, the one she'd been sipping from very slowly—lips barely touching the liquid—while the rest of us finished the bottle and started on the second one. It was possible she'd ordered her own glass simply to confuse any of the waitstaff who might have become an "anonymous source" for the paparazzi. I was about to ask her, when she grinned. "As adventurous as he is then. Good for you. Me, I'm a bit more traditional."

I thought of the last film I'd seen her in and the risqué photo spread to promote it. Maybe her idea of traditional and mine were not exactly the same. I shrugged.

"So my life's an open book," she said. "Utterly boring. I want to know all about you. Nigel says you're an academic."

"Yes. ABD, all but dissertation. Which is actually why I'm in England at all. Research."

"Oooh. I'll have to introduce you to Clare. She's one of my bridesmaids. Makes documentaries, and they always need good researchers." I filed the name away in my mind. It could easily be one of those throwaway offers of which nothing would ever come, but it could also be a lead to a job. Not that it was the career I wanted, but there was something reassuring about knowing my skills might be in demand outside the world of academia.

As Kate and I chatted, I was distracted by snippets of Nigel and Sebastian's conversation.

"Saw your mum, by the way," Nigel said. "Up at Stanton Hall."

Sebastian shrugged.

"Family is family."

"Have you met Seb's family yet?"

I blinked. And then realized Kate had changed the subject, had clearly realized I was struggling to listen to the men's conversation.

"Just Nigel and his parents."

"Ah."

I wanted to press. She couldn't just leave it at that. Someone had to talk, and if it wasn't going to be Sebastian, then Kate would do just as well. But our entrees were being placed in front of us, and our little side conversation disappeared into the ether.

WE WERE ALL, except for pregnant Kate, several sheets to the wind, Nigel particularly, when we stumbled out of the restaurant and out into the disorienting, carnivalesque world of London's Soho on a Saturday night.

Nigel pulled me back for a moment and leaned in close. "I wanted to apologize," he said, or slurred rather into my ear. "Seb doesn't have a history of serious relationships. But I like you."

I laughed.

It had been drunk talk, but that little exchange stayed with me. Even an hour later, when Sebastian and I stripped and fell onto the bed in a tangle of limbs, the alcohol making us more desperate for each other's bodies.

It was the alcohol, too, that made me breach the wall he always kept around him.

"Tell me about your family. About your mother," I pressed.

"Mmm?" His hot tongue swirled around my nipple, and I pushed him away, slid down until we were face-to-face.

"Your mother. Why don't you talk to her?"

"Not now." His hands crept back to my hips, and I slapped mine down on top of his, holding them still.

"Then when?"

"Mina." There was a wealth of irritation and impatience in his voice, and I was no longer nearly as tipsy as I had been. Maybe he wasn't either.

"This from the man who tied me up to get me to speak?" I said incredulously. "Is that what I need to do to you?"

He laughed, but the humor didn't quite reach his eyes. "It's a long story, Mina."

I shifted my hands to close over his wrists. Lifted his arms above his head. Interest flared in his gaze. Sexual interest, of course. His cock, which had started to soften with the talk of his mother, stiffened back to life against my stomach.

I straddled him, holding his arms above his head. He could easily throw me off, but that wasn't the point.

I narrowed my eyes. "You aren't getting off this easy."

I stared down at him, searching for something that would reveal him to me. I'd shown him nearly everything, but he was . . . he was a wall. Except for his lust. For the shifting of his hips under mine.

Nigel's words echoed through my head again. Maybe

this refusal to open up was the reason for Sebastian's lack of serious relationships, for his focus on sex alone.

Finally, he sighed and rolled his eyes up at the ceiling.

"Mina, it's not some great secret." Despite his casual words, his body was tense under mine. "My mom was having an affair, after my brother died. She told my father in the car. He crashed. She survived, and he didn't. I don't *not* talk to her, I just don't make any particular effort."

And there was the story, stark, unemotional.

"You blame her."

"We'd never been particularly close. She was much closer to my brother, James. But yes, I blame her."

I let go of his wrists. Slid my hands down his arms and then stroked the soft skin of his neck. I wanted to do more than that. Comfort him somehow, but that felt like I'd be crossing some other line.

I didn't have any words of advice. I could say he should forgive her, that life was short, that we had to focus on the present and the future. I didn't know his mother or his family and the dynamics that existed beyond those two sentences. And I wasn't all that close to my own family, even without the tragedy.

"Thank you for telling me," I said finally, opting for something that would disperse the tension. "You must not have wanted me to tie you up."

His lips quirked. "I have a far better idea."

An idea that involved drinking more and then continuing where we'd left off.

But I kept thinking about everything Sebastian hadn't

said, hadn't revealed. About his emotions, which were still so deeply tucked away.

Seb doesn't have a history of serious relationships.

That shouldn't bother me. After all, neither did I. In fact, if all flings and affairs were like this one, maybe I wouldn't long for one.

But I did long for a serious relationship.

And I did long for Sebastian. I swallowed down the errant thought. The one that didn't belong anywhere in my head.

I slid down Sebastian's body, my mouth ravenous in that way it seemed to get when I'd had a few drinks, and I took him in my mouth, loving his groans, his taste. Wishing he could fuck me even as I did this. Wanting him everywhere all at once.

When finally he pulled me up and fit himself between my thighs, I came at the first thrust. As my body shook between the orgasm and the movement of our bodies, my chest ached with a sense of loss that I wanted to understand, tears beading at the corner of my eyes.

Chapter Fifteen

THERE WAS SOMETHING about being Sebastian's plus one on a double date that made this affair we had feel more like a relationship. And despite my emphatic denial to Kate, there was a lump in my chest that grew with the hours because, as Nigel had said, Sebastian was not a serious-relationship sort of guy.

Not that I wanted one with him. Not that it was feasible, logical, or even desirable.

And once I knew there had been infidelity in his family, I saw a certain logic to his choices.

So, I threw myself into my work, determined to focus on that future Sophie so emphasized, on my dissertation. On reality.

Then . . . it happened. A breakthrough so basic and fundamental that I really should have had it months and months before. Another researcher on one of the many e-mail loops I was on asked if I had looked into the printer's partner, with whom he had split on acrimonious terms in 1830. Was it not possible that some of the records I sought, if they still existed, might be under his name?

I felt stupid for an instant, then threw the self-recriminations away and dove into the new line of inquiry. It might lead to nowhere, but this graduate student at the University of Glasgow, who was writing her dissertation on nineteenth-century Scottish publishers, was absolutely correct.

After splitting with Maddox, Wolford had married the daughter of a minor publisher, William Creighton, and joined forces. A good portion of Creighton and Wolford Ltd.'s papers were housed in the library of the University of London, where I'd already been several times. I scheduled an appointment with one of the archivists, explaining what I was researching.

I was cautiously optimistic. This process had been a roller coaster of emotions, and I was tired of the letdown after the renewed hope. I still had almost three weeks in England. So much could happen in that time.

LIKE GETTING CHAINED to a bed at Harridan House.

We were in a private room; the door was closed. But knowing that there were all sorts of peepholes in the club, I still felt exposed, blindfolded, nude, and spread-eagled, wrists and ankles restrained in velvet cuffs.

I wasn't certain what I was doing, but Sebastian had been insistent and persuasive, asking me to trust him. I wanted to trust him, for now. To do as he'd said and embrace the side of me that was engaged in the sensual world.

The mattress shifted, and I knew that Sebastian sat next to me on the bed. I could feel the heat of his body near my hip. I wanted to touch him, but I was stuck there, cool air kissing me in every open corner.

"You are so beautiful." His voice caressed me, then one hand followed suit, stroking me along my collarbone. Not being able to see him, not being able to move, made every other sensation that much more intense. I was so aware of sounds, of touch, of scent. Of Sebastian.

His hand drifted lower, to my breast, stroking in circles. He was my entire world, and anticipating what he would do next was my obsession.

His thumb slid across my nipple, before two fingers, or maybe three, closed over it, teasing, tugging. I sucked in my breath and squirmed. It was just a small touch, almost nothing really, but my breasts had never felt so sensitive. I could feel my other nipple, the one still as yet untouched, tight and rigid and wanting.

"Please," I whispered, not sure what I was begging for, unless it was more and faster and more.

"I like you this way," he said. His hand moved to my other breast and I sighed at that touch, at the way he cupped my flesh, the warmth of his skin spreading over me. "All mine."

The bed shifted, the air too and then more heat and his mouth hot and wet closing over my nipple, even as his hand squeezed my other breast, massaging it. His tongue swirled around me, and then his teeth grazed the sensitive skin lightly. I reached for his head, to thread my fingers through his hair, but my arm only moved an inch before the restraints made themselves known. I whimpered.

I felt his chuckle against my skin. His mouth moved, tongue trailing across my body, to give attention to my other breast. His movements were slow and decisive, lingering. My body tingled everywhere, from fingers down to my toes.

As if he knew, his mouth followed, touching all those places that thrummed with energy, all nerve endings awake. He kissed me up my arm, his tongue finding all the sensitive spots, the hollow on the inside of my elbow and where my wrist met my hand. Then back down. To my neck, my earlobe—to where my pulse flickered above my chest.

I had no sense of time, no sense of beginning or end. My world was his mouth, his tongue, and his hands trailing. He was everywhere and everything.

Finally, when I was lost in a drunken dream of colorful sensation, his breath eased over my sex. Then his fingers stroked across my flesh, down my wet slit, before spreading me open to the onslaught of his tongue, which flicked across the muscular little bundle of nerves.

I cried out, my voice high and needy. The more he played with me, licked me, brought me closer to the edge, the emptier I felt, the more I wanted him to fill me up.

"Seb," I moaned. "God, please!"

His answer was to thrust his fingers into me, and I sucked in air sharply before my hips jerked up, and my knees and my head arched back. Restrained as I was, I could do nothing but ride the wave of pleasure as his mouth and fingers kept torturing me.

Until he covered me with his body, thrusting hard and deep. The feel of his cock inside me was exquisite, and his mouth on my neck almost too much.

"I love the way you feel, squeezing me inside," he said roughly. Then he slid out again and I whimpered at the loss. I felt his hand at my ankle, and with a click, my leg was free, then the other one.

I moved them weakly, but he spread them apart again, grabbed me under my ass, and settled back inside with a decisive thrust. I strained against the cuffs that still bound my arms, and the bed shook with my frustration.

"No, not yet. You're not free yet," he murmured. I satisfied myself by wrapping my legs around his hips, urging him deeper. He groaned in a way that made me triumphant with pleasure.

He kissed me, and I devoured him. If only this–the endless rocking of his hips against mine, the tangle of our tongues–could last forever, then I didn't need to be free.

HARRIDAN HOUSE GAVE us a stage on which to play out our fantasies. From the flirtation with bondage to roleplaying. Emboldened by my new determination to embrace the honesty of our sexual desires, I wanted to please him even more.

One night, as we strolled through the club, we stopped in an open room to watch a woman sprawled out on a bed, alone, touching herself. Her body was different than mine, lusher and more voluptuous.

Her eyes opened and she turned her head to look at us and her gaze found mine. Then a lazy smile curved her lips. There was a clear invitation in that gaze. One that Sebastian seemed to be aware of as well. I remembered his words the night I first met Nigel; he'd prefer to watch me with another woman.

I glanced at him, tilting my head with an unspoken question. His lips parted in surprise, then his gaze darkened.

"You wanted to watch me with another woman," I said, voicing both our thoughts.

"Oh, I'd watch with pleasure." He let out a little laugh. "But Mina, you don't . . . only if—"

I didn't wait for him to finish the sentence. Instead, I stepped forward, shedding my cloak. The woman sat up, her smile broadening. Then she stood.

"I'm so glad you decided to join me. I've been . . . lonely."

I didn't ask why she hadn't joined one of the other groups of people elsewhere in the club or gone to the lounge to find a partner for the evening. I didn't care. I was about to do something I'd never imagined I would do, wasn't even entirely certain I'd enjoy, but I knew that it would bring Sebastian pleasure, and that in itself sent a certain warmth throughout my body.

I reached for her, tentatively, my hand sliding over silken skin that felt so different from any male's. I tangled my hand in her hair, and her body pressed against mine, breasts to breasts, thighs to thighs. Familiar and strange.

Then her lips touched mine. At first dry and then, as with any exploratory kiss with a new person, it increased in intensity. Lips parted, tentative touches of tongues to skin, to each other. She sucked my lower lip into her mouth, and I tried to forget who she was, where I was. Tried to focus only on the sensation. But my brain wouldn't stop working. She was a woman, and I had never been attracted to a woman before. Wasn't now really, despite the fact that my body was reacting positively to the physical sensation. Breasts growing heavier, warmth settling between my legs. And Seb was watching us. I opened my eyes a bit to peek over at him through the strands of this woman's sleek blond hair.

His face was slightly slack, mouth parted, eyes a bit glazed. His erect penis poked out between the folds of his cloak.

Desire hit me hard to the gut, that strange mix of nausea and intense arousal. I wanted him. I wanted him inside me, but the game I'd concocted was *this* woman. And she was still kissing me, her hands still wandering tentatively over my hips as if she had sensed I wasn't yet committed to our tryst. I deepened the kiss, took control the way I would have if she were Seb and I wanted to be in control. I moved away from her lips and kissed the line of her jaw. Held her at the small of her back as I molded my hand around the under curve of her breast, so similar to my own yet different, bigger, fuller, higher. I kissed down her skin, the way I had Seb's the night before, licking and seeking, trailing my tongue across the smoothness toward her breasts. I wanted desperately to feel her nipple in my mouth, to know how a woman tasted and felt. How I felt to Seb.

As I moved lower, I could smell the scent of her arousal, or was it mine? As I swirled my tongue around her left nipple, my right hand drifted down, brushed across the apex of her thighs, where her bare skin was hot under the pads of my fingers. She moaned and shifted in my arms, and the knowledge that I gave her pleasure turned me on even more. I shifted my head just enough to peek at Seb again, and instead of taking his cock into my mouth (just using that word to describe the length of him made me want him more), I sucked on her nipple. I slid my fingers down farther, felt the hot, moist, opening of her sex, where her lips parted, where her clitoral hood was slick with discharge.

I was thinking of her body all wrong. The parts too familiar, too clinical. Even as I stroked her gently, teasingly, in the way I liked to touch myself, my interest in her waned.

I didn't *want* her. I wanted Seb.

I parted the hot, slick folds of her skin and slid my second finger inside. I'd done this to myself before, marveled at the ridges and textures inside my body, and her body felt similar yet strange at the same time. Her body gripped my finger. I pulled out and in slowly in a mimicry of what I wanted Seb to do to me. The motion turned me on again.

I moved my oral attention to her other breast and slid another finger inside her. Shifted my hand a bit so that my thumb could work on her clit, push under the small hood and circle the sensitive skin.

She was moving in my arms, fidgeting, and I listened to her soft moans. How close was she to orgasm? She seemed content to let me pleasure her, one of her hands gently stroking my hair in a rhythm that I tried to mimic in my touch.

Her hips were shifting more wildly now, and I tried to keep my movements even, knowing how my own body worked, that even the slightest shift in rhythm could change the path of the build.

She sank down as she came, and I caught her, helping us both to the floor, to our knees, my hand still buried in her pussy (a word that felt right to me, finally, as I thought about this *other* vagina). Her lips sought mine, and we kissed wetly, deeply, her need that openmouthed, after-orgasm desire. I was fascinated by the feel of her convulsing around my fingers, and with her cradled in my arms, I kept thrusting lightly, trying to pull more sensation out of her. Wondered if I'd find I'd contracted some STD on my fingers.

Finally, she made a slight noise. Pushed my hand away. Under her black silk mask, she gave me a sleepy, boneless smile and then pushed me back so that I was lying on the floor. She ran her hands down the front of my body to where my knees were bent and pressed together. She pushed them apart.

I knew exactly what she intended: her mouth on my sex. I looked to Seb. He was watching so intently, and beyond him were several other men and woman, watching us. I didn't know how long they had been there. I didn't really care. But I knew what I wanted now.

I shifted slightly to get her attention, then shook my head. She looked confused, but I pointed at Seb, beckoned him over to me. She moved aside, and Seb took her place, undoing the clasp of his cloak to let the fabric drop.

I watched him kneel between my legs, his naked body fully on display, his *cock* jutting out in front of him. He pulled my hips up until I held them up, then with the length of him in one hand, he stroked up and down my heat, making it clear to both of us how wet I was. He was bare, and I wanted him to slide into me that way. Stupid as it was.

I could rationalize my desire any way I wanted, that I was on the pill, but condoms didn't protect against all STDs. Thanks to Harridan House, we'd both been tested recently, and aside from that moment with the woman, we'd been monogamous . . . but any which way I parsed it, unprotected sex was not wise.

A hand moved in front of him, holding out a condom. It was the woman, still so close to us though I'd forgotten her presence, gently enforcing one of the rules of Harridan House. Seb let go of me for a moment, and in the cold absence of his touch, I watched him tear open the package and roll down the thin barrier.

There were half a dozen voyeurs, as if this was some bizarre initiation ritual, and maybe it was. He grasped me by the hips again, fitted himself to me perfectly, parting me the way I had used my fingers on the woman earlier. Then he thrust.

I gasped and arched back at the feel of him inside me, stretching me, as if this were the first time and not yet another in a multitude of sexual interchanges we had shared. I looked up at his bare chest and sex-hewn expression with a sense of awe. Like my body was the sacrifice to some god of sex, a sacrifice that could only happen here, on the plush carpet of a strange, decadent club.

He slid out slowly, then back in just as slow, still holding my hips up. I closed my eyes and focused on the exquisite sensation, on the sounds of our bodies slick where we met. Everywhere he touched me, sensation was sharp, acute in a way it had never been with anyone else.

His mouth closed over my breast for an instant before I realized it was impossible. Before I shivered at the brush of silken hair across my chest. I opened my eyes and watched the woman in her black silken mask attend to me the way I had to her. Her mouth was hot and her tongue perfect. She sucked slowly, as if she were trying to match Seb's pace. I glanced up at him, found his jaw taut, tense with control. I couldn't have designed a better way to bring him to the edge, and I knew if we were alone, he'd be fucking me harder now. Instead, he was holding back, drawing this out. When she lifted her hand to my other breast, I closed my eyes again and gave in to the feel of four hands on my body, one mouth, one cock, to letting others be in control of my pleasure.

Her hand skimmed down my body, played with the V of hair between my legs, then down to right above where Seb and I were joined, to where my body throbbed and hummed, and suddenly I was shaking, lost in an explosion of color, sensation, and pleasure.

Then my hips were down on the ground and only two hands held me, and one hot male body leaned over my writhing body still deep inside me, his lips hot and open against mine. He urged my legs around him, and each continued thrust sent a new shudder through me, until he was shuddering, too, pulsing inside of me.

I held him tightly, loving the feel of us still joined, my body wrapped around his.

The sound of our ragged breaths hung in the otherwise silent room.

I turned my head languidly to the left. Found the room empty but for us.

We slowly disengaged, stood, weak-legged and well pleasured. We laughed a bit self-consciously at the experience, at the strangeness of being here, naked but for the cloaks and masks.

In one way I felt powerful, exuberant.

In another, I felt empty.

It had been all sex, fucking, skin against skin. If the night proved anything, it was that there was nothing special that stemmed from sex. If it was the basis of a long-term, romantic relationship, that relationship was inherently flawed. At one point, in my youthful idealism, oh so long ago, I had imagined a relationship with Sebastian. A real one that began with long conversations about our experiences, hopes, and dreams, and no sex until maybe the sixth date or longer.

I donned my cloak and excused myself to the restroom. As I walked, I was conscious of being nude, stretched open, damp between my thighs. In the hallway I passed a couple kissing, gained a brief impression of a woman's silver hair pulled taut into a high ponytail. Not that they would likely have cared if I had looked more closely. After all, voyeurism seemed to be the fetish most indulged.

But I wasn't so interested in other people. I was far too caught up in my own turmoil of emotions.

How far I had come in two years, from being shocked at Seb's suggestion of a threesome to initiating my own. Tonight had been the threesome we'd never had. I wasn't entirely sure why I had done it. Pushed myself to do it. Maybe subconsciously it was more of closing that thematic circle.

Or maybe I'd just wanted to see that look on Sebastian's face, the way he'd been slack-jawed at the sight of me with another woman. He'd been turned on watching me with the woman in the black silk mask, but I wasn't certain how I would have felt if it had been the other way around, if I'd been watching him fucking her. Maybe I wouldn't care, but somehow the seemingly greater potential for disease was too closely entwined with desire. Or rather a lack of. Maybe this would have been sexier in the seventies, before AIDS was a crisis, before there was antibiotic-resistant gonorrhea. Or maybe it was sexier in the Regency period, when Harridan House first began.

But supposing none of that was a concern (and those monthly tests the club demanded were supposed to help make it less of one). Supposing that we all knew for certain we were disease-free, how would I feel about watching him? Would it be a turn-on? Just how depraved was I? And did I really need to judge my sexual activities? Judge anyone's?

I found the washroom finally. Similarly to the one next to the spa, it was decorated in gilt and marble. Whoever designed this underground club had spent a fortune on it.

I cleaned up quickly and avoided looking at myself in the mirror on the way out.

I pushed the door open. The distant sounds of sex and laughter made it clear the party still continued. Seb was waiting for me, leaning against the wall in the otherwise empty hallway. A small wave of relief swept over me, as if I had been worried that maybe in these minutes away he'd found more entertainment.

When I reached him, he pulled me into his arms, buried his left hand in my hair, cradling my head. I stumbled against him, our cloaks half-trapped between us, half-parted so that in places we were pressed skin to skin.

"That was, without a doubt," he said softly against my ear, "one of the most erotic things I've ever seen or been a part of." It was less his words than the feel of him rising, semihard against my thigh, that sent a tendril of that acute, nauseous desire through my stomach. "And I must admit, I was... deliciously surprised. But I shouldn't have been. God, Mina, you're everything I've ever wanted."

I'd fed directly into some classic male fantasy. I'd done it intentionally. But what happened to sex between two people once the wall of monogamy was broken?

I pushed away from him, the emptiness overshadowing any thread of desire. What would happen when we left this idyll in Harridan House?

Who would I be when I returned home to the States?

Had I crossed a line that changed things, changed me, forever?

Chapter Sixteen

I KNEW SEB was puzzled by my moodiness on the way home. No doubt confused about why the sexually playful companion of earlier had disappeared. But he said nothing as, dressed in our normal clothes, bare-faced to the world, we passed through the streets of London.

I rested my head back against the seat, eyes closed.

It was late, and, in the morning, more research awaited me. For the first time since arriving in England, none of it excited me.

"I didn't ... *make* you do that?" he asked suddenly.

I opened my eyes and looked at him. He glanced over for a moment to meet my gaze before looking back at the road. Ugh! How did he have the ability to just look like this sweet, needy boy sometimes? Someone I wanted to protect. Someone who maybe cared about me the way a boyfriend would.

In some other universe, two years ago he might have been my boyfriend.

"You didn't make me do anything," I said tightly. Other than question everything about the way I live my life. Other than puncture my stupid, childish romantic idealism and propel me on a search for meaning in making sex as meaningless as possible. But I could no longer blame my own warped psychology on him.

"Then what's wrong?" He seemed relieved but still confused. Of course he was confused. *I* was confused!

"Just because you didn't make me fuck that woman doesn't mean I'm okay with what I did."

He laughed. "You hardly fucked her."

"I had my fingers up her cunt," I said crudely, suddenly angry. "I was penetrating her as surely as you penetrated me. That's how girls *fuck*." Then I added in an irate mutter, "Well, one of the ways."

"You have nothing to be ashamed of, Mina. It was beautiful. Erotic. You shared pleasure with another human."

Ashamed. I wasn't ashamed. Was I?

"The point was to turn you on, and I did," I said finally, brusquely, wanting the conversation over.

He was thankfully silent, and we didn't speak for the rest of the drive, not when he pulled into the garage or we rode the elevator to his flat. But when we'd crossed the threshold, when the door was shut behind us, he caught me and pushed me against the wall, gripping my wrists with his hands.

Breathless and surprised, I stared up at him.

His blue eyes were hooded and darkly intense as he pinned me with his gaze as firmly as his hands did.

"Mina, you turned me on, yes, but you turn me on just being you. I don't need to see you with another woman or take you to Harridan House to want you. That's just a fun diversion, a window into another life. I've wanted *you* since the first day we met."

I closed my eyes against the intensity of his expression, against the strangeness of being immobile against the wall. Against the way being trapped by him was making heat gather heavy between my legs.

Seb wasn't dense. Maybe it took him a while to figure it out, but he'd heard everything I'd said and not said.

"Okay," I choked out, knowing I needed to say something.

"What's *your* fantasy, Mina?" His voice was deep, and his grip loosened, his touch gentling, thumbs caressing the insides of my wrists. "What turns you on?"

I was turning to jelly in his arms, and he was asking me that. I opened my eyes and met his.

He growled deep in his throat. His grip tightened again even as his head swooped down, blocking the light, mouth claiming mine.

He let go of one of my hands and lifted my dress, pulled my thong to the side, and stroked me once, his fingers easily sliding between the folds of my sex, where I was wet and needy. Then my other hand was free, and he was down on his knees between my thighs, roughly pulling my thong down, mouth latching on.

This wasn't my fantasy, but I wanted everything he

was giving me, the rasp of his teeth against my sensitive skin, the swirl of his tongue—oh God—the thrust of his tongue inside me! I sagged against the wall and blindly reached for his head, fingers just grazing his hair. Then his mouth was gone, and he was pulling me down to the floor.

"Over," he said, and I shifted onto my hands and knees, willing to do anything he wanted for the feel of him inside me. He pressed tight and rubbed himself against me, the fabric of his shirt rubbing against my backside, the length of his cock stroking my sensitive skin. I arched back, wanting more, wanting him in. He leaned over me, his mouth close to my ear. "I'm not going to use a condom. I don't want anything separating us."

"Yes." I nodded, too, my heart pounding in anticipation, until I felt him bare and parting me. I gasped as he slid in, at the electric feel of skin to skin, of the thrust of his body deep within mine, no barriers.

"God, you feel good," he said, his hands grasping my hips, the urgency of his movements making my elbows bend till the parquet floor was cool against my cheek.

The thrusts and retreats found a rhythm, relentless. My skin tingled all over, nipples tender against the fabric of my lace bra, and yet I centered there in the muscles that gripped him, that reacted to every impulse of his body.

"Touch yourself," he ordered. I reached back to do so, and my clitoris was slick under my fingers, making it hard to find the touch I knew I liked. My fingers distracted me, too, made orgasm the end game. I moved my hand back to the floor, focused on him, on the delicious sensation of him inside me over and over again, on the quickening of his breath, the way his body tightened against mine. Pleasure was sharp within me, and when he came, deep inside, I felt everything his body shared with mine. Then I came, too, surprising me, as if my body and his were having a conversation of which I was merely an observer.

I would have collapsed fully on the floor, but Seb held my hips tight against him, still thrusting gently against me, wringing every last shudder of passion out of us both.

I savored the feel of his semen sticky on my thighs, of the damp between my legs being a mixture of both of us. Risky and stupid, perhaps, but I felt . . . closer to him. More his.

And maybe that was the stupidest thought of all.

A CERTAIN DESPONDENCY claimed me, infected everything I did. In contrast, Sebastian seemed to need to have sex with a new frequency and fervor, which meant that we spent the evenings that week lingering in bed for hours, barely speaking in a language other than sex.

I met with the archivist, and she helped guide me through the Creighton and Wolford collection. I spent days there, poring over documents, few of which had been cataloged. There was a letter from Anne Gracechurch to Wolford, apparently in return to one of his own, in which she declined an offer to publish with him instead of his erstwhile partner.

I wondered about her loyalty to Maddox when it seemed as though Wolford was offering more money than she had previously received for any of her work, especially since she had expressed time and again in letters that if not for the need for income, she would not write another word.

But there was no mention of what works Wolford had asked about. The date was after the last of the three Mead books, and there was no overt mention of James Mead.

When I'd finally exhausted the collection, I hit a wall. I spent the next day on the couch, hair unbrushed, breakfast and lunch forgotten.

I was not going to find the connection. Certainly not before I returned back to the States. I'd been through every known link to Anne Gracechurch and then some.

I would be leaving with that failure.

All too soon, I would be departing the crazy world in which I'd been ensconced here in London. In Sebastian's apartment

It was August. I stared at the computer screen, at my university's Web site, rereading all the deadlines and regulations for what should be my last year as a graduate student. I'd been avoiding this, living in the present only, trying to ignore the future and the inevitable parting.

I'd fallen hard for Sebastian.

Which was ridiculous and stupid because all that we had was sex. His casual words two years earlier had turned me into a female version of him, sexually experimental, as I'd proven that last night at Harridan House. These last weeks had been one big grand experiment in depravity.

So maybe I needed some sort of finale. Some other

boundary to cross. Then I could go home, go back to my life. No regrets.

I was still in the tank top and shorts I'd been wearing all day when he walked in the door. Six o'clock already?

He looked tired and somewhat rumpled, and something about that made me jump up off the couch and go to him as he dropped his leather bag on the chair of the kitchen table.

"Long day?"

"Nothing unusual," he brushed off. Which was usual too. Despite his decade of schooling in the States, he had never lost his reticence to share his emotions. He reached for me, his eyes lighting up. I still wasn't entirely certain how he'd spent the six months before we'd hooked up celibate, as it was clear that he found release from the stress of his job in sex. He worked hard and played hard.

I was just play.

Which I hadn't minded this summer. After all, he was play for me too.

And more, that tiny voice in my mind reminded me.

"Well, I hope you're not too tired," I said suggestively. His thumbs pulled on the waistband of my shorts, stroking the skin underneath.

"I think I can manage."

"Mmm." I pulled away. "Not here though. I thought we could go back to Harridan House."

Like that, the air between us shifted. The mood charged with something other than sexual anticipation. He didn't seem excited by the idea. In fact, he looked at me warily, as if he suspected there was something more to my suggestion.

"Mina, is that really what you want? After the other night?" When I didn't answer right away, torn between wanting to admit that it wasn't and needing to go there, needing to find a way to say good-bye. "Harridan House was an obsession for me, a diversion from work, which, as much as I enjoy it, is stressful. So I wanted to find out what had happened to it. But simply because the club still exists doesn't mean I need to go there every night. Or ever again."

I laughed. Seb was saying this. Seb, who had started me on my journey of sexual adventure. Now he was willing to step away from it all? After he'd spent the equivalent of a new car on our membership?

"I enjoyed it," I said finally. "And you're right. Shame is stupid." He smiled, like I was a pupil who had at last learned her lessons. "Even more, I'm going home next week."

He frowned. "I can't believe it's so soon."

"Yeah," I muttered. "Anyway, you asked me what my fantasy is," I said, as if he hadn't satisfied it the night he'd thrust inside me bare, flesh to flesh. Had continued to do so every time since.

He relaxed slightly, interest sparking in his eyes. "Whatever it is, I'll do my best to satisfy it."

A shiver ran through my body at his expression. I knew he would satisfy me. Amply. He was a wonderful lover and I'd miss his touch. I'd miss his body.

"Okay. Good."

He stepped closer, took me into his arms, and one hand cupped my cheek. I melted where he touched me, my lips parting. All plans nearly falling away at the desire to have him naked and inside me now, here.

"What's your fantasy, Mina?"

I blinked.

He ran his thumb over my lips, and I grabbed at it with my teeth. He pushed inside my mouth, and I sucked on his thumb greedily, using my tongue to run up and down his skin.

He made a small sound, half groan, half sigh and then pulled his hand away, threaded it through my hair, and lowered his mouth to mine. He destroyed me with his tongue and his teeth, searching, pulling, until I wasn't certain where his mouth began and mine ended.

His other hand was grabbing at my butt, fingers sliding between my legs, under the fabric of my shorts, nearly touching my core through my cotton underwear. Each movement pushed me closer against him. I lifted one leg to wrap around him, to feel him hard and hot against me.

Almost three months and I was still insatiable. But there wasn't anything about him and his body that made me feel uncomfortable with mine. He was so at ease, so natural.

One of his fingers slid under the cloth of my panties, and I moaned into his mouth as he stroked me. I was always so impatient and greedy, wanting to be penetrated, filled, at the first touch.

But this was one of those days when Seb wanted to torture me, to go slow.

Then his hands were on my waist, running up and down from the slight indent to the curve of my hips, finger closing down almost painfully.

He broke the kiss, his breath coming in short gasps.

"It's not enough," he said, "It's never enough." His mouth closed over my neck, and down.

My eyes burned damply, and my chest ached, his stupid, careless, meaningless words making me yearn for something that was impossible and foolish.

"Stop," I whispered gruffly. "Let's save this for the club. I want you *there*."

He pulled away slowly, taking deep breaths. "Mina, if you're doing this because you think that's what I want—"

"What about what I want?" I interrupted him. "I didn't ask to be a member, but I am, and now I want to go back. I want to make the most of the time I have left."

He looked confused, or maybe distraught. I didn't know, and I looked away so I wouldn't have to analyze how he felt or worry about his emotions. What mattered now was me. Saving myself.

Chapter Seventeen

IT WAS AUGUST but I was shivering as we walked from Sebastian's car to the storefront that hid one of Harridan House's entrances. So innocuous to walk through the highly respected wine shop, flash the silver bracelet with its iconic design, and make our way into the storage rooms and down to the concealed door. And through there, down a plush, carpeted hallway to more stairs, which took us down to one of the entry halls.

It was a bit cooler down in the club, but that didn't account for the tremors that racked my body, the chattering of my teeth that I fought desperately to conceal from Sebastian. But he kept glancing at me as if he thought something was wrong, as if he didn't want to be here, and each solicitous look made me angrier. Warmed me up until the trembling ceased.

We didn't touch each other as we changed, stored our clothes in the gilt lockers, padded out in our velvet slippers, cloaks, and masks. Tonight was different, and Sebastian knew it, even if he didn't know why.

"After you," he said, gesturing in front of him. He was pensive, even quieter than usual as I led him through the warren, peering briefly in the open rooms, searching, and then finally stepped into the lounge.

"Drinks first," I explained, but even as he ordered for us, I scanned the room.

I found what I was looking for. She was young, maybe a bit younger than me and her lips and jaw, the only reveal beneath her more concealing half mask, made me think of a model. Her brown hair flowed loose and tousled over the back of her chair, and her cloak was artfully askew, revealing. In front of her was an empty glass and another one half-full of something that from this distance looked fruity.

Whether she was awaiting someone or simply alone, I knew she was perfect. I left Sebastian at the bar and walked over to where she sat on the velvet sofa. Perched next to her, letting my own cloak fall where it might. I was past any physical insecurity. This was how seduction was done here at Harridan House. It began with the physical reveal, and then the request. I'd seen it happen more than enough times to know. But still, finding the practiced words was hard.

"I'm Mina. Would you like to join us?" I said simply, gesturing to Sebastian, who was walking toward me with our drinks and that concerned crease on his forehead.

"Flor. What's your kink?" she asked, and from the accent, I knew she wasn't British. Spanish, maybe?

"I want to watch him with someone else."

I ignored Sebastian as he sat down in the chair across the table even though I knew he must have heard what I said.

The woman turned to study him. Then smiled.

"I have a friend who is late. Male. He'll join us."

It wasn't exactly what I wanted, but if this woman wanted two men instead of one, it wouldn't really make a difference to me.

I nodded. Looked to Sebastian, who had a small, deceptive smile on his face. He was pretending. Fine by me. He'd be turned on soon enough.

I took a sip of my drink, welcoming the familiar taste, the warmth of the alcohol that would make everything easier.

"Come." The woman said, taking charge. "I know exactly which room."

"*This* is what you want?" Sebastian demanded as we followed her from the lounge, his voice low.

"Yes," I insisted. "And she's gorgeous. *I'd* fuck her." I kept my tone light, flirtatious, trying to remind him of how hot he'd found the sight of me with another woman the last time.

"Mina." He spun me around, and I was up against the wall with him kissing me, deeply, devouring me. "It doesn't have to be this way," he murmured. "Let's go."

I closed my eyes against his kisses, against the words. Tried to find the strength to convince him that this was what I wanted.

"Hmm." Sebastian broke away and we both looked at Flor. "Perhaps you don't just want to watch?"

I swallowed hard, trying to clear my head. "No, that is what I want." I shot a challenging look at Sebastian. His lips tightened before he nodded once.

She raised an eyebrow and reached for Sebastian. He looked at me a moment longer, his eyes full of doubt, then he stepped into her embrace, head lowering, mouth finding hers.

The kiss was tentative at first, each of them learning each other, then it deepened, the natural result of continued sensation. Sebastian's hands ran down the outside of her cloak, molding it to her body, exploring her curves.

Flor broke away. "You know how to kiss." She gestured to the right with her chin, to an open door. With a teasing glance, she slipped the cloak from her body and passed over the threshold. Sebastian looked at me again. I forced an encouraging smile.

His lips set, and he turned from me, entered the room. I took a deep breath. Looked around the dimly lighted hall with its maroon walls and gilt sconces. Then I followed them inside.

I hung back by the door, observing. The room was sparse, as far as Harridan House went: a bed, a velvet chaise, a table with towels, and the ubiquitous crystal bowl of condoms and lube. The rooms never seemed dirty, and I imagined a secret army of cleaning elves that crept into each room after every encounter, disinfecting and wiping away signs of previous use.

Finally, I turned my eyes reluctantly to Sebastian, who was kissing Flor again, and she was unfastening his cloak, running her hands down over his arms. I could see his erection sandwiched between them and, knowing how that hardness would feel against my skin, sucked back a moan. I didn't want to watch. I wanted to be her. In his arms.

But I'd wanted this pain. This jealousy. This final breaking of any pretense at monogamy, or at there being anything to our relationship but the exploration of pleasure and sex.

It wasn't slow between them. They'd found their rhythm, their chemical attraction, and Sebastian was all over her, hands, mouth, almost rough in his intensity. She was moaning rather loudly, and I wondered if that was for me or if she was usually that vocal.

I watched the moments of sex progress, her manicured hands closing over his cock, his fingers disappearing inside her pussy. The two of them descending onto the bed.

I was turned on despite myself, moistening my lips with a sudden need to be licking, kissing, participating. I slipped my hand between my legs and touched myself, my fingers slipping slightly. Yes, I was undeniably wet.

Then Sebastian broke away to grab a condom, and he looked at me. Whatever he saw must have satisfied him because he sent me a beautiful smile, and I found myself smiling back.

She took the condom from him and ripped it open, slid the latex down his length, grinning up at him as she did. She pulled him down, over her, and I moved forward slightly to get a better view as he pressed against her pink folds, pushed forward, and slid inside.

My sex clenched, and I moved my fingers more vigorously on my clit.

I felt the pressure of the room change and glanced to my right to see a man, casually nude, enter the room. I had only the briefest impression of salt-and-pepper hair, tanned skin, a muscled, fit body, before I turned back to watching Sebastian. To watching his pale buttocks move rhythmically. I'd never had this view of him before, and I admired the power of his body.

"I see she couldn't wait. She's stunning, isn't she?" the man said. His words confirmed for me that he was the one Flor had meant to meet. There was no jealousy in his voice, only lust and admiration. Even as my insides were all bunched up in confusion, I had to agree. Her head thrown back, her body taut with growing pleasure, and with Sebastian's beautiful body pumping into her, she was gorgeous. *They* were gorgeous. I was disturbed and aroused all at once. And my fingers still moved between my legs but more slowly now. I hoped the voluminous folds concealed my actions.

I hardly noticed at first when the man's hand rested on my arm over the cloak, but then he pulled it to the side and pressed himself against me as his hand rounded over my breast. I stood frozen in shock, my own hand stilled over my sex. His mouth closed over my shoulder. His fingers pulled on my nipple. It felt good and wrong all at once. I had no idea who this man was, had hardly glanced at him when he'd entered the room. Knew only that he was at least passably attractive and likely a good decade or more older than me

"Don't stop touching yourself," he said. He moved to stand fully behind me, pressing himself against my back, and through the fabric of the cloak I could feel him hard against my backside, nestling against the crack of my buttocks. After a moment's hesitation, my fingers moved again. I focused on watching Sebastian and Flor, on letting this stranger's hands and body simply be an accessory to my pleasure.

I'd learned well over the last two years, and this last week more profoundly, that pleasure needed no deeper emotions. His other hand closed over my other breast and as he massaged me, kneading my flesh, his tongue licking the sensitive skin of my neck, I watched Sebastian slide in and out of Flor. Their movements were increasingly frantic, and the room was filled with moans—mine, Sebastian's, Flor's. The stranger's hips rocked against me, and his hand moved down, closed over mine, then took over the manipulation of my clitoris. The warmth and pressure had me gasping. It was almost too much, too confusing, the visual stimulation and the physical, feeling pleasure but seeing Sebastian several feet away engaged in his own.

He looked over his shoulder and our gazes caught. With the silk mask obscuring his expression, I only felt the intensity of it, could only wonder at what he was thinking, before he turned back to Flor.

Everything seemed to speed up after that. His thrusts,

her screaming pants, the stranger's fingers. Sensation was rising in my body, my legs were shaking, and then I was crying out and bucking, my head arched back.

I leaned back heavily on the man for support and forced my eyes open. Sebastian and Flor had found their climax, too, and Flor was looking at me—or looking at the man behind me—while Sebastian had rolled off her to his side and stared up at the ceiling.

I was swept up in strong arms and laid gently on the lounge. My mind a confused blank mess, I watched the anonymous man whose hands had pleasured me step toward the bed. Watched lips move, new greetings or words of some sort be exchanged, then Flor's lips close over the man's penis. Which was just as thick and erect as it had felt against me.

Sebastian's hand twitched, and his head turned to look at Flor and the other guy. My gaze flickered down to where his now-flaccid penis was still wrapped in the wet condom. I looked away.

What the hell was I doing here? What had I done? I buried my head in my arms and tried to make sense of it all, to remind myself it didn't matter. That now I could go home and leave this all behind.

It wasn't Sebastian's fault. Maybe tonight had been the catalyst, but there was no doubt I was someone who liked sex, who could enjoy the touch of anyone regardless of emotional connection. At the same time, I still had some ideals. Deep down I wanted monogamy. Wanted all these sexual desires to stay in the bedroom with just one man.

And I'd proven to myself fully that that man couldn't be Sebastian.

"Let's go." Sebastian's hand on my arm, pulling me up was rough and his voice tight, as if he were angry.

I stumbled to my feet and struggled to keep up with him, wondering at his sudden change in demeanor. He'd thrown the condom away, but he hadn't even bothered with his cloak, and we were walking fast down the corridors, past other members.

HE LED ME into the spa, ripped the cloak from my body, and pulled me into one of the showers. He turned the water on and it came down us strong and hot from both jets. Poured shower gel on his hands and wiped it first down my body, then his. I yanked my sodden mask off and stared at him.

"What's wrong with you?"

"What's wrong with me?" he demanded, taking his own mask off. I shrunk back at the fury on his face. "What the hell was that little scene about? 'I'm just going to watch' and then his hands all over you."

I looked at him incredulously, the fact that he was jealous dawning on me.

"How was that different than that woman the other night? Because it was a man? I was in the middle of watching you fuck some other woman, and you have a problem with a man getting me off with his fingers?"

"We didn't agree to it!" Sebastian's voice was raised, and I'd never heard him like this before. I looked out through the smoky glass, wondering if anyone else could hear us. He grabbed my chin and forced me to look back at him. "It has to be mutual, Mina. I didn't do anything you didn't agree to. You did."

"So what's the big deal?" I pushed his hand away, trying to disguise the fact that I was terrified inside, that I felt guilty, like I'd done something horrible. Of course, I'd planned to do something that would end things definitively between us, but . . . this was different. Sebastian was angry with *me*. "It was just sex. It's just about pleasure. No different than what we've been doing all summer."

His face went red, and then I was really scared. I reached for one of the disposable loofas and poured more shower gel on it, trying for some normalcy.

"Just sex?" He shook his head. "You think that's all that's been going on between us?" He ran a hand through his hair as if he'd pull it out, as if he were in agony. As if I'd maybe misjudged everything.

Except I hadn't.

"Yes. What does it matter?"

"Not matter?" He grabbed me again, by the shoulders this time, and I flinched at his touch. "What the hell—" He let go of me and grabbed a loofa too. We washed ourselves off in angry silence, punctuated every so often by Sebastian ejecting half a phrase: *I can't believe—How could I have been—*

"Don't," I said finally, desperately. "Don't pretend we were having a *relationship*. Like this ever would have lasted past next week, when I go back to New Jersey and these last months fade into the past. You chose Harridan House. You're the one who wanted to come here and had sex just now and—"

"I fucked that woman because you wanted me to. You told me it was your fantasy, Mina." His eyes flitted back and forth, searching my face, and the anger suddenly seemed to leach out of him. He shook his head. "But I made the mistake I thought I was too smart to make. I didn't take into account the power of fear. I believed you because I never imagined you were just too much of a coward to face up to the fact that maybe something real is happening between us."

"Something real? You think this is real? You pay me—"

"I paid you to do research!"

"What do you want from me?" I glared defiantly at him, daring him to say something different, something braver than he claimed I was.

He stared at me. His light blue eyes open. Thinking.

In our silence, the sound of the water hitting our bodies, pounding against the tile, grew thunderous. I turned the silver knob and reached for the towels in the shower's little antechamber.

"I . . . I want you to stay."

My hands fell to my side, and my face felt slack. I turned back to stare at him, wide-eyed. I'd dared him, but I'd never imagined he might actually say it. Actually want it.

He reached for me again, but this time not angrily, one hand curving behind my head, where my hair was wet and plastered against my body. I blinked away the sudden hot tears.

"I don't want it to be all about sex. I want more." He pulled me in, and I went, stunned and distraught, flat against his chest. But he wasn't done yet. He just kept torturing me with words. "I want you to do what you need to do, finish your degree, and then find a position here."

"We barely know each other, Seb, sex aside." What I said as I shivered in his embrace was true. Maybe two years before we'd had half a dozen deep conversations, and these last months we'd had countless more, pushed each other, been as physically close as two humans could be, but that wasn't the basis for me to make some permanent transatlantic move. Or for Seb to do so either. At least not for a while.

"What I know is that we were *friends*, Mina, and I fucked that up," he said. "But I was lucky enough to get a second chance. There's more here. There's been more the whole time." He shifted and cupped my face in his hands, lifting my chin up, everything about this touch painful in its gentleness. I stared into his eyes. Water dripped from his hair onto my forehead, my cheeks, hot like tears. "I want to give us the chance. I want you to stay."

Stay. Stay. Stay. The word echoed in my head, emptying me of all other thought, of speech. I was aware instead of sensation, of his fingers stroking the line of my jaw, like he could make me say something.

My brain snapped back to life with a flood of impossibilities. I grabbed two towels, nearly throwing one at him, and then wrapped myself in the other one, taking another for my hair as I left the shower.

So he'd been thinking of me as his girlfriend. And why shouldn't he have? I'd been the ideal one for him this summer. Willing to cede independence and decisions for the chance to finish my work. Willing to sleep with him, to explore the kinkier side of sex, or at least what was kinky to me. I'd now witnessed sexual acts and fetishes that I had no desire to experience for myself.

And what would a relationship between the two of us in the future be? A continued membership at Harridan House as long as all acts were agreed upon in advance? Would Sebastian really be satisfied without that?

Would I?

I didn't talk to him as we dressed and returned to his apartment, but everything inside me ached. We got ready for bed in that same silence, and when I finally climbed under the covers, I lay on the edge, turned away from him.

Until he invaded my space and held me close, his body so familiar. My stupid attempt to prove I couldn't be with him meant nothing. The activities in which we'd engaged at Harridan House—*that* was just sex. But here, in the privacy of his flat, his bed–this was more, no matter who else he'd fucked.

We didn't agree to it. It has to be mutual, Mina. Sebastian's twisted morality was not so twisted. Was fundamentally honest. He'd tried to stop us from going to Harridan House. I was the one who had pushed. He'd humored me.

Of course, he hated anything that smacked of cheating, that broke trust. I knew his family history. A dark fog of disgust enveloped my thoughts, my chest. I'd been trying to protect myself and I'd given no thought to his emotions. I'd been selfish and cruel.

I lay there in the endless dark, thinking, feeling, reexamining everything with the frantic pace of desperation. He was awake, too, his thoughts as silent and raging as my own.

Finally, at some point in the night, he let go of me and fell onto his back with a sigh.

I flipped over to face him. His arm was over his head, forearm resting against forehead, but at my movement, he turned his head to look at me. Questioning. Waiting.

"I thought if you slept with someone else, I'd break everything between us."

His lips pressed together tightly, but he didn't speak.

"When he touched me, I was going to move away. And then I thought that that act, too, would make everything more final."

"Sex without emotional attachment *is* just sex," Sebastian said. "You and me? We like physical pleasure. If you'd even wanted to fuck him, I would have dealt with my own jealousy. But it's infidelity that breaks relationships."

"I know," I said quickly. "*Now*, I know. But . . . I didn't know we had a relationship."

Sebastian looked back up at the ceiling, squeezing his eyes shut.

"You're right," I continued. "I'm a coward."

"Mina." His voice sounded ragged, like he was struggling to speak, and it hurt me. Hurt me the way his anger at Harridan House had terrified me, had made me realize I didn't want *him* to be angry with *me*. "We've had a relationship since the first day we met."

"Why did you never ask me out?"

"I don't know." He opened his eyes and sat up. In the dark, I could just make out the pale outline of his body, arms resting on his knees, head in his hands. "No, I know why. Because I was immature. I'd only be in the States a few more months and I wanted to fuck around. I knew you were the kind of girl . . . you'd be my girlfriend. Things would be complicated."

Girlfriend. That's what I'd wanted. And what had I imagined? A long-distance relationship based on sweet romance? But who knows what would have happened if we'd acted on our attraction back then. Maybe I hadn't needed a "wild" year of my own to be his sexual match. In fact, the concept went against all my ideals, my feminist ideology. Just as all the shame I'd held all those months should have gone against it as well. It was all too complicated. My actions and motivations, and Seb's, didn't fit neatly into some theory. This wasn't school, or research. I wouldn't be writing some dissertation that analyzed everything to death.

And analyzing this right now, when all I needed to know was that he wanted to be with me, with only me, was stupid.

So the question remained: What did I want?

"I'm sorry. About tonight. It wasn't fair to you. None

of it." It wasn't enough of an apology. Nothing would be.

He didn't answer, but the uneven sound of his breath filled the space between us.

"I have to go back," I continued. "I have a TA position for the fall. In the spring . . . maybe I could come for a month or two while finishing up my dissertation, but then I'd have to return to defend it, finish everything up. Then, who knows where I'll get a job. It would be long-distance . . . which is what you didn't want."

"Right." A single word. Was I convincing him? I wanted him to lie back down and grab me and tell me none of the obstacles mattered. That we had to try. That what we had was bigger than distance.

But was it?

Was it for me?

"But maybe a few months long-distance, and some time together in the spring, and we'll know." I hardly felt like myself speaking, voicing the tentative desire to try. "We'll know it's . . ." I took a deep breath. "It's love and worth compromising for. Worth shifting our lives to make it—"

He was on top of me so fast, the movement took my breath away.

"—work," I gasped, finishing the sentence even as his hands held my wrists by the side of my head and his body pressed mine down.

"So that's a yes?"

"Yes."

"Good. Because it *is* for me. And I want to give this . . ." *Love?* Was this love for him? I hardly heard what else he said as the word spun through me, warming me in a way nothing else had ever before in my life. Wondrous. Is that what he meant? He *loved* me?

His mouth lowered to mine, and the kiss tasted like love. Like a promise. Like tenderness. Like something that my stupid attempt at words couldn't even describe. When he let go of my wrists to cup my face, I wrapped my arms around him.

When he finally slid inside me, I wrapped my legs too. I pressed my body to his as tightly as I could, lifted my hips to keep him as deep as possible. His movements were slow and infinitesimal, but each shift sent tremors through me, unfurling, colorful ribbons of sensation and emotion. And I said with my lips what my heart and mind were too full to say.

Love.

Chapter Eighteen

"Would you like another drink?"

I turned my head lazily to squint at Sebastian in the bright afternoon sun.

"Mmmhmm," I agreed, and watched him walk off, admiring the way he looked in his swim trunks. After a week in Cannes in the south of France, we both were more tan than usual. And after a week of getting-reacquainted-with-each-other's-body sex, I still wanted to pull closed the curtains of the cabana, strip off my bikini bottoms, and fuck him here.

I was starved for sex after the last four months without him, and I had no way of knowing if this summer would be all we had for another half year. We were celebrating regardless. Celebrating the fact that I'd finished my PhD, that I'd had an article on the overwhelming similarity between James Mead and Anne Gracechurch (using forensic and computer analysis, and framing it as a mystery) accepted for publication. That we could even spend this time together. Things were good.

We'd managed to make long-distance work these past nine months, in part thanks to some creativity with Internet video calls and in part due to the efforts we'd made to see each other. Although I'd had to miss Nigel and Kate's wedding, Sebastian had joined me in November for my sister's. I'd spent half of December and all of January in London, working on the final stages of my dissertation before I submitted it for defense. The backup version. I also used that time to follow more clues into the Mead-Gracechurch connection. While I had decided to cut my losses as far as the dissertation, I was still determined to find the missing link.

During those weeks, we'd even visited Harridan House one more time just to walk through the halls as ghosts, to fuck in one of the rooms. We hadn't closed off the future to any possible fantasies that might creep up, but bringing other bodies between us at this fragile point felt like an invasion of the world we were hoping to build. The love.

The life that would be that much more difficult to maintain if I accepted the fabulous tenure-track position I'd been offered in Ohio. If it had been New York, or Chicago, or San Francisco even, then Sebastian could have been the one to sacrifice, move to a department stateside since he was still years from breaking out on his own. Instead, I had postponed accepting, which I knew meant other candidates were also waiting with bated breath. But there were still two postdoc positions that were due to be announced soon, and there was always the possibility of working as a researcher at that documentary-film company in London for which Kate had mentioned one of her bridesmaids, Clare, made films.

Sebastian returned with two bright pink, fruity drinks, the glass wet where the frozen drinks sweated in the sun. On the beach, his predilection for scotch appeared to be subsumed by a taste for tropical, sugary drinks.

He sat back down next to me on the triple-wide sun bed. Handing me the drink even as he leaned in for a kiss. On my bare breast. I'd taken to the topless sunbathing easily after all those nights at Harridan House. And there were all these little perks, even if "lewd" behavior on the beach was frowned upon.

"We should close the curtains," he murmured.

"We should," I agreed. I put my drink down on the table beside me, bestirred myself from the outdoor bed, and undid the ties that kept the canvas back. Tugged the edges closed. Then I climbed back on and crawled over to Sebastian. Straddled him.

The feel of him hard under me had me bite back a moan. Discretion was necessary.

My fingers rested over his nipples, which hardened under my touch. I looked down at his face, a study in pleasure. He reached his hands up to the strings on the side of my bikini bottoms and tugged. The fabric fell away and his fingers replaced it, reaching for me, cool on my hot flesh. I shifted up a bit, pulled his shorts down to free his cock.

Positioned myself over him and eased down, sucking in my breath as always at that first delicious feel of his parting me, stretching me, joining us.

We moved slowly, hips undulating, and I leaned forward to meet his open mouth. In the instant before, I saw his face, saw that look in his eyes. The one I hadn't understood last year. The one I'd tried to deny.

This wasn't just sex. I felt that too.

No. It was more.

So much more.

Something worth keeping.

About the Author

SABRINA DARBY has been reading romance since the age of seven and learned her best vocabulary (dulcet, diaphanous, and turgid) from them. The day after her wedding she woke up with an idea for a novel and she's been writing romance ever since. She is the author of *On These Silken Sheets, The Short and Fascinating Tale of Angelina Whitcombe,* and *Entry-Level Mistress.*

Visit www.AuthorTracker.com for exclusive information on your favorite HarperCollins authors.

Give in to your impulses . . .
Read on for a sneak peek at three brand-new
e-book original tales of romance
from Avon Books.
Available now wherever e-books are sold.

THE GOVERNESS CLUB: CLAIRE
By Ellie Macdonald

ASHES, ASHES, THEY ALL FALL DEAD
By Lena Diaz

THE GOVERNESS CLUB: BONNIE
By Ellie Macdonald

An Excerpt from

THE GOVERNESS CLUB: CLAIRE

by Ellie Macdonald

Claire Bannister just wants to be a good teacher so that she and the other ladies of the Governess Club can make enough money to leave their jobs and start their own school in the country. But when the new sinfully handsome and utterly distracting tutor arrives, Claire finds herself caught up in a whirlwind romance that could change the course of her future.

What would a "London gent" want with her, Claire wondered as she quickened her pace. The only man she knew in the capital was Mr. Baxter, her late father's solicitor. Why would he come all the way here instead of corresponding through a letter as usual? Unless it was something more urgent than could be committed to paper. Perhaps it had something to do with Ridgestone—

At that thought, Claire lifted her skirts and raced to the parlor. Five years had passed since her father's death, since she'd had to leave her childhood home, but she had not given up her goal to one day return to Ridgestone.

The formal gardens of Aldgate Hall vanished, replaced by the memory of her own garden; the terrace doors no longer opened to the ballroom, but to a small, intimate library; the bright corridor darkened to a comforting glow; Claire could even smell her old home as she rushed to the door of the housekeeper's parlor. Pausing briefly to catch her breath and smooth her hair, she knocked and pushed the door open, head held high, barely able to contain her excitement.

Cup and saucer met with a loud rattle as a young man hurried to his feet. Mrs. Morrison's disapproving frown could not stop several large drops of tea from contaminating her white linen, nor could Mr. Fosters's harrumph. Claire's heart sank as she took in the man's youth, disheveled hair, and rumpled clothes; he was decidedly *not* Mr. Baxter. Perhaps a new associate? Her heart picked up slightly at that thought.

Claire dropped a shallow curtsey. "You wished to see me, Mrs. Morrison?"

The thin woman rose and drew in a breath that seemed to tighten her face even more with disapproval. She gestured to the stranger. "Yes. This is Mr. Jacob Knightly. Lord and Lady Aldgate have retained him as a tutor for the young masters."

Claire blinked. "A tutor? I was not informed they were seeking—"

"It is not your place to be informed," the butler, Mr. Fosters, cut in.

Claire immediately bowed her head and clasped her hands in front of her submissively. "My apologies. I overstepped." Her eyes slid shut, and she took a deep breath to dispel the disappointment. Ridgestone faded into the back of her mind once more.

Mrs. Morrison continued with the introduction. "Mr. Knightly, this is Miss Bannister, the governess."

Mr. Knightly bowed. "Miss Bannister, it is a pleasure to make your acquaintance."

Claire automatically curtseyed. "The feeling is mutual,

The Governess Club: Claire

sir." As she straightened, she lifted her eyes to properly survey the new man. Likely not yet in his third decade, Mr. Knightly wore his brown hair long enough not to be following the current fashion. Scattered locks fell across his forehead, and the darkening of a beard softened an otherwise square-jawed face. He stood nearly a head taller than she did, and his loosely fitted jacket and modest cravat did nothing to conceal broad shoulders. Skimming her gaze down his body, she noticed a shirt starting to yellow with age and a plain brown waistcoat struggling to hide the fact that its owner was less than financially secure. Even his trousers were slightly too short, revealing too much of his worn leather boots. All in all, Mr. Jacob Knightly appeared to be the epitome of a young scholar reduced to becoming a tutor.

Except for his mouth. And his eyes. Not that Claire had much experience meeting with tutors, but even she could tell that the spectacles enhanced rather than detracted from the pale blueness of his eyes. The lenses seemed to emphasize their round shape, emphasize the appreciative gleam in them before Mr. Knightly had a chance to hide it. Even when he did, the corners of his full mouth remained turned up in a funny half-smile, all but oozing confidence and assurance—bordering on an arrogance one would not expect to find in a tutor.

Oh dear.

An Excerpt from

ASHES, ASHES, THEY ALL FALL DEAD

by Lena Diaz

Special Agent Tessa James is obsessed with finding the killer whose signature singsong line—"Ashes, ashes, they all fall dead"—feels all too familiar. When sexy, brilliant consultant Matt Buchanan is paired with Tessa to solve the mystery, they discover, inexplicably, that the clues point to Tessa herself. If she can't remember the forgotten years of her past, will she become the murderer's next target?

She raised a shaking hand to her brow and tried to focus on what he'd told her. "You've found a pattern where he kills a victim in a particular place but mails the letter for a different victim while he's there."

"That's what I'm telling you, yes. It's early yet, and we have a lot more to research—and other victims to find—but this is one hell of a coincidence, and I'm not much of a believer in coincidences. I think we're on to something."

Tears started in Tessa's eyes. She'd been convinced since last night that she'd most likely ruined her one chance to find the killer, and at the same time ruined her career. And suddenly everything had changed. In the span of a few minutes, Matt had given her back everything he'd taken from her when he'd destroyed the letter at the lab. Laughter bubbled up in her throat, and she knew she must be smiling like a fool, but she couldn't help it.

"You did it, Matt." Her voice came out as a choked whisper. She cleared her throat. "You did it. In little more than a day, you've done what we couldn't do in months, years. You've found the thread to unravel the killer's game. This is the breakthrough we've been looking for."

She didn't remember throwing herself at him, but suddenly she was in his arms, laughing and crying at the same time. She looped her arms around his neck and looked up into his wide-eyed gaze, then planted a kiss right on his lips.

She drew back and framed his face with her hands, giddy with happiness. "Thank you, Matt. Thank you, thank you, thank you. You've saved my career. And you've saved lives! Casey can't deny this is a real case anymore. He'll have to get involved, throw some resources at finding the killer. And we'll stop this bastard before he hurts anyone else. How does that feel? How does it feel to know you just saved someone?"

His arms tightened around her waist, and he pulled her against his chest. "It feels pretty damn good," he whispered. And then he kissed her.

Not the quick peck she'd just given him. A real kiss. A hot, wet, knock-every-rational- thought-out-of-her-mind kind of kiss. His mouth moved against hers in a sensual onslaught—nipping, tasting, teasing—before his tongue swept inside and consumed her with his heat.

Desire flooded through her, and she whimpered against him. She stroked his tongue with hers, and he groaned deep in his throat. He slid his hand down over the curve of her bottom and lifted her until she cradled his growing hardness against her belly. He held her so tightly she felt every beat of his heart against her breast. His breath was her breath, drawing her in, stoking the fire inside her into a growing inferno.

He gyrated his hips against hers in a sinful movement that spiked across her nerve endings, tightening her into an almost painful tangle of tension. Every movement of his hips, every slant of his lips, every thrust of his tongue stoked her higher and higher, coiling her nerves into one tight knot of desire, ready to explode.

Nothing had ever felt this good.

Nothing.

Ever.

The tiny voice inside her, the one she'd ruthlessly quashed as soon as his lips claimed hers, suddenly yelled a loud warning. *Stop this madness!*

Her eyes flew open. This was *Matt* making her feel this way, on the brink of a climax when all he'd done was kiss her. *Matt.* Good grief, what was she thinking? He swiveled his hips again, and she nearly died of pleasure.

No, no! This had to stop.

Convincing her traitorous body to respond to her mind's commands was the hardest thing she'd ever tried to do, because every cell, every nerve ending wanted to stay exactly where she was: pressed up against Matt's delicious, hard, warm body.

His twenty-four-year-old body to her thirty-year-old one.

This was insane, a recipe for disaster. She had to stop, now, before she pulled him down to the ground and demanded that he make love to her right this very minute.

She broke the kiss and shoved out of his arms.

An Excerpt from

THE GOVERNESS CLUB: BONNIE

by Ellie Macdonald

The Governess Club series continues with Miss Bonnie Hodges. She is desperately trying to hold it together. Tragedy has struck, and she is the sole person left to be strong for the two little boys in her care. When the new guardian, Sir Stephen Montgomery, arrives, she hopes that things will get better. She wasn't expecting her new employer to be the most frustrating, overbearing, and . . . handsome man she's ever seen.

When he reached the water's edge, Stephen stopped. Staring at the wreckage that used to be the wooden bridge, he was acutely aware that he was looking at the site of his friends' death.

Images from the story Miss Hodges had told him flashed through his mind—the waving parents, the bridge shuddering before it collapsed, the falling planks and horses, the coach splintering, George's neck snapping, and Roslyn—God, Roslyn lying in that mangled coach, her blood pouring out of her body. How had she survived long enough for anyone to come and see her still breathing?

Nausea roiled in his stomach, and bile forced its way up his throat. Heaving, Stephen bent over a nearby bush and lost the contents of his stomach. Minutes later, he crouched down at the river's edge and splashed the cold water on his face.

From where he crouched, Stephen turned his gaze down

the river, away from the ruined bridge. He could make out an area ideal for swimming: a small stretch of sandy bank surrounded by a few large, flat rocks. Indeed, an excellent place for a governess to take her charges for a cooling swim on a hot summer day.

Stephen straightened and made his way along the bank to the swimming area. A well-worn path weaved through the bush, connecting the small beach to the hill beyond and Darrowgate. The bridge was seventy meters upstream; not only would the governess and the boys have had a good view of the collapse, the blood from the incident would have flowed right by them.

No wonder they barely spoke.

Tearing his gaze from the bridge, he focused on the water, trying to imagine the trio enjoying their swim, with no inkling or threat of danger. The boys in the water, laughing and splashing each other, showing off their swimming skills to their laughing governess.

Stephen looked at the closest flat rock, the thought of the laughing governess in his mind. She had said she preferred dangling her feet instead of swimming.

His mind's eye put Miss Hodges on the rock, much as she had been the previous night. The look on her face after seeing his own flour-covered face. Her smile had been so wide it had been difficult to see anything else about her. He knew her eyes and hair were certain colors, but he was damned if he could name them—the eyes were some light shade and the hair was brown, that he knew for certain.

And her laugh—it was the last thing he had expected from her. He was in a difficult situation—not quite master but regarded as such until Henry's majority. For a servant, even a governess, to laugh as she had was entirely unpredictable.

He shouldn't think too much about how that unexpected laughter had settled in his gut.

The image of Miss Hodges sitting on the rock rose again in his mind. The sun would have warmed the rock beneath her hands, and she would have looked down at the clear water. She would laugh at the boys' antics, he had no doubt, perhaps even kick water in their direction if they ventured too close. Her stockings would be folded into her shoes to keep them from blowing away in the breeze.

Good Lord, he could almost see it. The stockings protected in the nearby shoes, her naked feet dangling in the water, her skirts raised to keep them from getting wet, exposing her trim ankles. The clear water would do nothing to hide either her feet or her ankles, and Stephen found himself staring unabashedly at something that wasn't even there. He gazed at the empty water, imagining exactly what Miss Hodges's ankles would look like. They would be slim, they would be bonny, they would—

Thankfully, a passing cart made enough noise to break him out of this ridiculously schoolboy moment. Inhaling deeply through his nose, Stephen left the swimming area and made his way back for a closer look at the ruins.